CROW CHILDREN

CROW CHILDREN

James Dixon

GUPPY BOOKS

CROW CHILDREN
is a GUPPY BOOK

Manufacturer: First published in Great Britain in 2025 by
Guppy Publishing Ltd, Bracken Hill, Cotswold Road, Oxford OX2 9JG

www.guppybooks.co.uk

Represented by: Authorised Rep Compliance Ltd,
Ground Floor, 71 Lower Baggot Street, Dublin D02 P593, Ireland

www.arccompliance.com

Text copyright © James Dixon, 2025

978 1 916558 465

1 3 5 7 9 10 8 6 4 2

The rights of James Dixon to be identified as the author
of this work have been asserted in accordance with
the Copyright, Designs and Patents Act 1988.

All rights reserved. No part of this publication may be reproduced,
stored in a retrieval system, or transmitted in any form or by
any means, electronic, mechanical, photocopying, recording or
otherwise, without the prior permissions of the publishers.

Papers used by Guppy Books are from well-managed
forests and other responsible sources.

GUPPY PUBLISHING LTD Reg. No. 11565833

A CIP catalogue record for this book is
available from the British Library.

Typeset in Minion Pro by Falcon Oast Graphic Art Ltd
Printed and bound in Great Britain by CPI Books Ltd

For Betty and Norma

One

Dustin Marr came up to her the day after she and Mum arrived in Crawford. She was standing outside St Francis' Academy, getting a first look. It backed onto a broad field that swept up to the forest's treeline. She turned and walked up to the forest, stood there staring at it, at the wooded hills that strode along the horizon, and he came up to her.

'You Ava?' he asked. He prowled, came over to her and looked down at her and squinted. 'Ava Bridger? The new girl?'

She looked at him and nodded. They both stood shoulder to shoulder looking up at the forest together. The blackforest, people called it. Crows swirled around above the trees.

Ava stole sidelong glances at Dustin Marr and blushed. He was tall and gaunt, as skinny as she had ever seen anyone and a couple of years older than her, maybe fifteen or sixteen. Dark hair framed his cheeks and he seemed to wear a permanent scowl, though he was handsome, beautiful, even, with high cheekbones and sparkling blue eyes. His skin was like marble, Ava thought, pure white and almost glowing with it.

'Ava Bridger,' he repeated. His voice was soft. He smelled of ash and something animal.

'Yeah,' she said. 'So what?'

'An outsider,' he said. He smiled to himself and bared his teeth. Ava shook her head.

'My mum grew up around here,' she told him. 'My nana and pop live here. Their parents did, too, going way back, I think. And I've been coming here forever in the summer holidays and that.'

'So why have you moved back?' Dustin Marr asked.

Ava swallowed and looked at her feet. Then she looked up and squared her shoulders. There was no avoiding it. People were always going to ask. She felt her cheeks burn and her eyes burn and she took a deep breath and said the words she hated saying.

'My dad died a couple of years ago. Mum wanted to move back home. It's cheaper here, she says. She can afford it better. And she wanted to be closer to my nana and pop. We're staying with them for a bit. Until we find our own place.'

Dustin Marr grunted.

'Your nana and pop are good people,' he said quietly. 'Specially your nana.'

'Yeah?'

Dustin Marr didn't respond. He just carried on staring up at the woods for a little while.

'What do you hear?' he asked her eventually. 'When you stand near the woods?'

Ava didn't understand. 'What are you talking about?' she asked.

Dustin Marr nodded up at the trees. 'What do you hear?'

She listened out. Crows called to one another up in the trees. Plenty of other things squawked and screeched.

'I dunno. Some birds. Woodland noises.'

'Anything else?'

'No.'

He nodded. 'For now, maybe.'

She wondered if he was mad. She took half a step back in fear as he reached into a pocket and pulled something out, held it out to her on his open palm.

'Look,' he said.

She was relieved. It was nothing dangerous. It was beautiful, in fact, a crow's head carved from a dark and rich looking wood.

'I whittled it myself,' he said. 'And I lacquered it and varnished it so that it wouldn't spoil.'

'Yeah?'

He held it out for her. 'Take it. It's yours.'

'Really?' She felt herself blushing again.

He shrugged. 'I can always make more,' he said. He nodded at the blackforest. 'There's plenty of wood, isn't there?'

'Yeah. I suppose so.'

'You know anyone yet?'

'Not really.'

'That's OK. You'll soon know all you need to know. I'll see to that, Ava Bridger.' He looked at her and his eyes flashed. 'You should come along with some of us one day,' he said.

'Come where?'

Dustin Marr nodded up at the woods again. 'I've got a place,' he said. 'We do a ritual there. Spooky stuff, you know. We talk to the crows. Some say it's bollocks but they're idiots.'

'The crows?'

'Yeah. They're like messengers to the dead. From the dead.'

'Yeah?'

'Yeah.'

And that was that.

She showed Mum and Pop the carved crow's head later on.

'I know the family of old,' Pop said. 'And your nana knows him well, Dustin Marr. Used to babysit him when he was a little boy. It doesn't surprise me, this kind of talent.'

'It looks kind of sinister,' Mum said.

'That doesn't surprise me either,' Pop replied with a small chuckle. 'Nothing about that lot would surprise me very much.'

Two

Dad fell down dead one day at the site. Mum got a call from the foreman. Then she screamed. Then she cried. Ava had mostly been angry. Furious, even. Sometimes it blotted everything out, or so it felt to her. Sometimes everything felt pointless. Life and the whole lot of it.

'You're depressed,' Mum had told her. She took Ava to see a doctor back home before they moved. He gave her some pills to take every day which made her feel rubbish, disconnected. A couple of times she went a few days without taking them. She would put them in her pocket in the morning and then flush them down the loo when she had a chance. It would make her feel good to be rebellious like that.

You're depressed. It's natural. Only natural, people often said.

It doesn't feel natural, she often thought.

She flushed the whole pack of pills in the end. All of them. Mum wasn't happy. The doctor wasn't happy.

'It's reckless, foolish, to do something like that without proper medical supervision.'

'So supervise me,' Ava said. 'I'm not taking those pills any more. You watch me if you want.'

'Yes, well.'

So the doctor had agreed to it without much of a choice.

'A trial, to see how you get on.'

'Sure,' Ava said. She smiled at the doctor. They both knew she wasn't going back on them.

That was over a year ago and she was getting on better, or at least had been until they left home. She missed her old flat. She missed her old school and her old friends, though there weren't many of them, especially towards the end. Sometimes she missed Dad, wanted to speak to him. She never got to say goodbye. He just left for work one morning and never came home again and the thought of it made her shake with rage sometimes. Other times she felt so incredibly unhappy. The sense of pointlessness weighed her down.

Ava got into a fight at school, at her old school, a

few months ago. The rage took over that day. She didn't remember it very well, only that a couple of girls in the year above had made some kind of snide remark. They joked about Dad and Ava went for them. She hurt them. Mum picked her up from school and then sat her down a few days later and cleared her throat. She looked nervous as she told Ava that they would be moving.

'Back home,' she said. 'To my home, Crawford, with Nana and Pop, where I grew up.'

'Why?' Ava asked.

'We need it,' Mum said gently. 'I need it. I need to be close to Nana and Pop right now. And honestly, I can't afford to keep us here, not without ... you know, your dad's wages as well as mine. One salary alone doesn't go far enough these days, and Crawford's cheaper.

'We can move in with Nana and Pop for a bit, then get a house nearby and help them as they get older. It will be nice to be able to see them all the time. I can get a new job around there, and there's a decent school there ... my old school, St Francis'.'

She looked at Ava nervously.

'Love, what do you think?'

'Whatever,' Ava said. She walked away and swore

under her breath as she went, loud enough for Mum to hear, quiet enough that she could pretend she hadn't.

So they came, they arrived. Ava sat alone on her bed in her new room in Nana and Pop's little house and felt frightened and abandoned, dumped in this new place. She wanted to speak to Dad right then. She just wanted him to hold her one last time.

Ava heard a scrabbling at the window. Something screeched outside and she jumped. There were a couple of crows at the window. One of them was sitting on her windowsill and rattling its sharp beak against the glass. *Tap, tap, tap*, it hammered away. The other swooped and swirled through the air and came in close and went out again.

'Go away!' Ava shouted.

She looked through the glass. Her own reflection shimmered there with dark hair hanging lank and a pale face frowning. She looked just like Mum but with Dad's grey eyes. She glowered and her reflection glowered back, and she thumped on the glass. The crow on the windowsill fell backwards and flapped its wings and rose up into the air to glare back at her. The other swooped past and Ava smacked the glass again until they both fled.

Three

Pop and Nana were delighted to have them. They were delighted to have Ava there, especially Nana. She struggled to recognise Ava at first. Her memory was going and it shocked Mum.

'I didn't know how bad she had got,' she told Ava afterwards. 'Your pop didn't tell me how far gone she was.'

Pop sat whispering to Nana and it was like the lights were slowly coming on behind Nana's eyes as Ava watched. She was stocky limbed and wire haired where Pop was tall and slim and balding like a giant tortoise out of its shell. Ava thought that Nana looked grumpy and mean, but eventually she smiled. She grinned and her whole face lit up and softened and looked more like it always had when Ava was younger.

'Oh Ava, love,' she said. 'But look how quickly you've grown up.'

Nana liked to go walking around town, but she wasn't allowed out in case she got lost.

'Nonsense,' she snapped. 'I've lived here my whole life. How could I ever get lost?' But she still had to have someone with her all the time and Mum told Ava to take her out.

'Go on, love,' she said. 'It'll be a good chance to get to know the town a little better.'

'Fine,' Ava said, though she thought she knew all she needed to about the town.

She resented being told what to do. She resented having to take Nana out at first, having to basically babysit her. Except that in the end she had a nice time. Nana seemed to know everything when she wasn't in a forgetful mood, every corner of the town, with more stories than Ava knew anyone could keep in their heads.

'Every tale tall and small,' she said with a throaty laugh.

The town was all tightly packed terraces and close lanes. 'Every brick and stone full of stories,' Nana said. 'A rich history. Industrial history, mostly, though that's more your pop's cup of tea than mine.'

They hunkered down stoically, all those rows of houses, or so it seemed to Ava. They were all a lot like Nana and Pop's own house. No front gardens, just doors leading straight out onto the street with small yards in the back. Alleyways cut behind each, through every block. It all seemed less miserable with Nana by her side.

Ava laughed at Nana's jokes and listened to her stories. Crows followed them sometimes. Other times they sat in trees or on the tops of fences, watching. They looked mean and Ava glared at them.

'They can be buggers,' Nana told her. 'But not fully. They're decent things if you get to know them a bit. Not like most people say.' She told Ava stories about them. 'Folks see them as bad omens these days,' she said. 'But they were sacred to our ancestors. Sacred to the Celts who used to roam the woods and hills around here. Sacred but bloody if you take my meaning. They were thought to escort the dead to the afterlife.'

'Yeah,' Ava said. 'That's what Dustin said. Dustin Marr. That they're like messengers to the dead.'

Nana nodded.

'Something like that. And he should know. I taught him all the old stories when he was a boy. It's good to know he remembers them. That he was paying attention.

'They were symbols of evil, but a necessary evil,' she carried on. 'A part of the natural way of things. Not a curse.'

She stopped to catch her breath, which she had to do every so often as she got tired from walking and talking. But soon enough she was off again, transporting Ava away with her stories.

'It was only when folk began to settle down, when they became industrialised, you might say, that they lost their marbles and started calling crows all sorts of silly names. They began to talk a lot of rubbish.

'They're carrion birds, you see. They eat the dead. But that's all well and good. The dead nourish them and so help new life to flourish, if only folk had the wit to see it.'

She looked at Ava levelly.

'Do you know what a flock of crows is called?' she asked. Ava shook her head. 'A *murder*,' Nana said. 'A murder! Can you imagine? A murder of crows ... but then, people are such fools at times ...

'And the crows are so much more, according to the oldest stories ... Like I said, they escort the dead to the afterlife. They're there, waiting for us on the other side, whatever the other side is. And they guide us to whatever comes next – heaven, the otherworld, islands in a vast sea ... Valhalla, maybe ... who knows? But they take us there. Though they demand payment for their services.'

'What do you mean?'

'They guide us in exchange for our stories, our memories. They are atavistic, true to their own natures. They guide us and take our stories because it's in their nature to do so. Carrion birds to their core, feeding off the dead. Eating flesh, taking memories, taking all that we are to nourish themselves. Because let's be honest, we all live in stories, don't we? And those stories are all too often stories of suffering. But we suffer through living, and in surviving the suffering we find meaning, and our stories take that meaning and show it back to us, show it to the world.'

'Really?' Ava was sceptical.

'Of course!' Nana said. 'And this gives us our *why*, why we do what we do, why we should, why we will. And anybody who knows and understands their *why* can bear to live almost any how, any way. That's the power of stories, the stories we tell each other, the stories we tell ourselves.'

Ava thought of Dad, walking along to the next life, telling the crows all his silly old stories. She thought of Dustin Marr's words. *We speak to the crows* ... She daydreamed a little, thinking about talking to the crows, telling them stories. Hearing their *why*, figuring out if there was any meaning in any of it at all, like Nana said. Probably not, she thought. It's probably just rubbish.

They carried on for a bit. They got to the river and followed it down to a large lake welling up at the town's outskirts.

'Do you know what Crawford means?' Nana asked. Ava shook her head. 'It means *crow's ford*, where crows live by the water. But few remember stuff like that. Only old biddies like me. And of course, old Corbie himself.'

'Who's Corbie?'

'Ah,' Nana said. 'There's a story. Corbie ... he's the leader of the crows, their spirit, love. The spirit of the town itself, some would say.'

But Nana was beginning to grow tired. She drifted off as they walked towards home. Ava thought that she began to look like a little lost girl. 'We played make-believe when we were young,' she said in a singsong voice after a while. She sounded cheerful but her eyes were solemn and sad.

'We played in the river in the summer and pretended old Corbie watched us the whole time, kept an eye out for us. Oh, the fun we had, didn't we, Evelyn?'

Evelyn was Mum's name, but Ava realised that Nana was talking to her. She didn't know what to do. She just smiled awkwardly and nodded and hurried up her footsteps a bit. Nana was staring ahead vacantly, looking thoroughly lost by the time they got back to their street. Pop was sitting on the front step waiting for them with a worried look on his face.

'That's it, Ava love,' he said as he stood up. 'Thank you, my dear. I've got her now.'

He took Nana's hand and led her inside, so gentle that it was like he was handling glass.

Four

Ava's new form tutor Miss Faulkner met her by the school gates. People bustled all around but she smiled kindly through it all. She was tall so had to stoop slightly as she intercepted Ava. Golden ringlets swished around her head as she moved.

'Hello, love,' she said. Her voice was warm and rich.

'Hi.'

'Well, then,' Miss Faulkner carried on. 'Welcome to St Francis'. I'm sure you'll fit right in. Come on, let me show you to our form room.'

Miss Faulkner led Ava into a smaller building that squatted next to a larger main one. She took her upstairs and stopped outside a slightly faded, peeling door, and stood aside for Ava. 'This is us. Room D13. That's D block, first floor, room 3. Like in a hotel.'

'OK, then,' Ava murmured. She didn't know what else to say. Nerves bundled tight in her stomach as the noise of hundreds of students rose around her and made her feel small.

'Come on. Let's find you a seat,' Miss Faulkner carried on. She glanced at a seating plan on her desk and smiled. 'Ah, good, there's a space free here. You'll be next to Josie . . .'

It was a space on a table near the back. Ava took her seat just as the door crashed open and thirty or so others began to crowd in, pushing and banging. It was overwhelming. Ava's heart beat hard and she started to sweat lightly. Lots of people craned their necks to look at her as they took their own seats. Some even twisted in their seats to see who the new girl was, and Ava scowled. She didn't know what else to do.

A girl plonked herself down next to her with a huff. She was pretty and fair and she shot Ava a look before crossing her arms and staring pointedly in the other direction. Josie, presumably. She soon started chatting with a couple of others, ignoring Ava completely. They all looked at Ava at one point before covering their mouths and laughing.

Ava burned. She seethed. She felt the anger rising in

her, but Miss Faulkner called everyone to order before anybody could say or do much else.

'Come on, enough now, quiet,' she said. Peace nestled over the room as she stood at the front and got ready to take the register. Everything stayed calm enough as she called out names, getting thirty-odd responses of 'yes, miss'. Ava's name was one of the first and she nearly choked when Miss Faulkner called it out. She just about managed to reply and Miss Faulkner shot her a sunny smile before carrying on to the next name.

'We're very lucky today,' Miss Faulkner said when she was done with the register. 'We have someone new joining our form. I'd like you all to join me in welcoming Ava Bridger to St Francis'.'

'Hiiii, Ava Bridger,' the class said in a bored, sing-song voice.

'Ava,' Miss Faulkner said. 'Why don't you stand up and tell us a little bit about yourself.'

Ava felt herself blush. Everybody turned as one to look at her expectantly. The girls around Josie sniggered. Ava didn't know what to do or say put on the spot like that.

'Come on, love,' Miss Faulkner said. Ava could have killed her.

'OK, well . . .' she muttered. She stood up and her mind went completely blank. Everyone was looking at her, but it was like she had forgotten every word she had ever known. She felt her throat constrict. She was scared and she didn't know what to do with the fear and she didn't know what to say, but she didn't want the class to know how scared she was, so she had to say something, anything.

'I'm Ava,' she began. She croaked and cleared her throat and began again. 'I'm Ava. And I came here with my mum because my dad died a couple of years ago and Mum wanted to be closer to my nana and pop who live here.'

She caught her breath. Everyone was looking at her a little puzzled. Miss Faulkner looked worried.

Well sod you, Ava thought, glaring at her new teacher. *You put me in this position.*

But she knew what it was all about. That puzzlement. That worry. Nobody wants to hear about anything like that, dead parents and the like. It made most people uncomfortable talking about death. They often just looked at her blankly when she talked about Dad and said 'sorry' or something stupid like that and changed the subject before anybody got too embarrassed.

She flailed around for something else to say as the moment drew on and people just sat and stared. Miss Faulkner opened her mouth, about to take the situation in hand at last. Then somebody said something. Ava didn't know who it was, didn't catch what was said, but everybody immediately began to snigger.

You bastards, she thought. She burned. She felt it closing in on her, like she couldn't breathe, and she balled her fists.

Then she saw a face. One face amongst it all as Miss Faulkner shouted and scolded. The face was pretty, dark with green eyes and framed in coppery curls. It belonged to a girl across the room who looked at Ava, not laughing, not smiling. The girl was dressed in an artfully shabby uniform with open shirt over white T-shirt and feet in bright red trainers poking out from under her desk. She had bright bangles at her wrists and heavy make-up on her face. She met Ava's eyes and smiled kindness, and all that rage suddenly vanished.

Five

Dustin was leaning on a wall outside the main school building, watching people as they walked past. Ava felt her heart begin to beat quickly as she went over to him.

He had a length of wood in one hand. He had carved one end into the likeness of a skull. The rest was mostly smooth, though he had etched jagged letters along it which looked kind of cruel to Ava, though she quite liked them. The whole thing was just about longer than his forearm and he was spinning it around like a baton.

'Runes,' he said as she went up to him and he saw her looking at the letters. 'Viking runes.'

'What do they mean?' she asked.

He shrugged. 'All sorts,' he said. 'They're cool, aren't they?'

'I guess.'

The skull watched her. It winked in the bright sunshine. Dustin pointed the skull towards a nearby window. It was an art classroom and there were some wooden figures on the windowsill inside, crowded in amongst paintings and bits of pottery and all sorts. A couple of the wooden figures were half-bird, half-man. Ava went over for a closer look. She peered inside, squinting a bit against the sun's glare on the windowpanes. The two half-men were both lunging forwards as if about to take flight, or perhaps as if to pounce on some unwitting prey. They had the torsos and arms of men, with bestial legs, cruel, beaked heads, and ragged, widespread wings sprouting from their backs. A third carving stood nearby, a large skull fashioned from some kind of knotty wood. It had a deep cut running vertically across one eye socket.

'All mine,' Dustin said, following her over to the window.

'Yeah,' she said. They were all beautiful in the same dark way as him. 'It's very you.'

'What does that mean? You think they're rubbish?'

'No.' She straightened up and looked at him. 'I like them. They're just, you know, kind of scary too.'

The art teacher appeared inside the classroom. She saw Ava looking at Dustin's carvings and she frowned deeply. She glared at Dustin through the window and Dustin glowered in return and swore under his breath.

'What is it?' she asked.

'Some people,' he said. He spat on the ground and turned his back on the classroom.

They walked together for a little while. Crowds parted before them as they both glared at everyone. Ava enjoyed it. She enjoyed the scared looks on their faces as they saw the two of them, strange and scowling. Dustin threw his short, carved staff in the air so that it spun.

'Anyone looking for anything,' he said.

'What?'

'My ritual. Like I said. It's for anyone looking for anything,' he repeated. 'What are you looking for, Ava Bridger? Cos I've seen the way you look. Like you can't quite see what's right in front of you. Most people can't. Blind as anything. That's what my mum always says, and I reckon she's right. But you look like you know it at least. You know it like I know it.'

'Shut up,' she said. She wasn't comfortable with anyone talking like they knew her, like they knew what she was thinking. He had no idea who she was. 'I don't know what you're talking about.'

'Ha!' Dustin laughed, then he looked at her. 'Not many people in this school would talk to me like that. No one else, in fact.' He threw the skull staff. It spun in the sunlight and he caught it. 'Did you keep hold of that crow head I gave you?' he asked.

'Yeah,' she said. 'It's on my bedside table.'

She blushed, embarrassed saying it.

Dustin simply nodded, though. 'That's something at least,' he said.

'When's the next ritual?' Ava asked after a minute or so.

'Friday after school, if you're not chicken.'

Ava told him to shut up again. Dustin shook his head this time. He pointed the skull at her and squinted down the staff's length.

'Careful,' he said.

Ava swallowed.

'Fine,' she said. 'But I'm not chicken.'

'Good. Meet us out by the woods. Same place I found you the other day, near enough. You'll see us.'

Then he was off, twirling his staff once more.

Six

She saw the girl from her form when she got home that afternoon, the one who hadn't laughed. It turned out that she lived right next to Nana and Pop. Ava had been thinking about her all day and figured she looked familiar.

Ava saw a woman out walking a little dog along the street as she got back to Nana and Pop's.

'Come on, love, Grimble won't bite,' the woman told Ava. She smiled. Ava stooped and tickled him behind the ears. He immediately began to make a husky noise in the back of his throat.

'That's him grimbling,' a voice said. Ava turned and saw the girl beaming from her front door. It felt like the whole world lit up as Ava watched her toothy grin.

'He's really called Trevor, but that's a terrible name so we ditched it,' she said. 'Called him Grimble instead.'

Ava just nodded.

'I'm Robin,' the girl added. 'And this is my mum.'

Her mum smiled at Ava. 'You can call me Jeanie.'

'We'll be friends,' Robin carried on. 'I'll knock for you in the morning and we can walk to school together.'

Ava just kept nodding. She caught herself doing it like an idiot and Robin laughed lightly and headed inside as her mum carried on her walk with Grimble.

Ava was sitting up in her bedroom later that evening with her window open. It overlooked Nana and Pop's small backyard and the alleyways beyond. A beautiful voice floated in through the open window. Ava looked out and saw Robin in her own yard below. She was sitting singing by herself with her eyes half-closed. Her voice was clear and sad and joyful all at once and Ava sat there listening until Jeanie called Robin in.

Seven

It was the middle of the night and Nana was walking along the landing. She was quiet for a moment. The whole house seemed to hold its breath. Ava pulled her duvet up around herself and tried to ignore it all. But then she heard Nana speaking, confused.

'Corbie, you beast! Where have you gone off to?'

'For God's sake,' Ava muttered. She sighed and got up. She tiptoed out of the bedroom and saw Nana at the end of the hallway. Pop's snores grated at the air. He was oblivious to it all. Mum showed no signs of stirring.

'Nana!' Ava hissed. Nana turned and frowned at her.

'Corbie? Is that you? I see you with those spirits. Come, come. You be gentle with them. They've been through enough.'

'No, Nana. It's me. It's Ava.'

'Hush, now, Evelyn. You're talking nonsense.'

'Jesus, Nana. Come on.' Ava stepped forwards and frowned. 'I'm Ava.'

'What?' Nana tensed. 'Who's that then?'

'Ava, Nana. Your granddaughter.'

'Evelyn's girl?'

'Yeah, Nana, that's me.'

'Oh, well I knew that,' Nana snapped. Then she seemed to Ava to soften, to relax as she came back to herself. 'Oh, my sweet child, my love,' she said. 'I've just been looking for Corbie.'

She shook her head.

'No,' she corrected herself. 'No. I've been being a silly old biddy.'

She smiled.

'Come on, love,' she said. 'Let me see you back to bed. Then I'll turn in myself. Maybe I'll even stay put this time. Not that his nibs in there would notice either way.' She nodded at her bedroom door. Pop's snores continued to hack and haw, and Nana laughed.

'Come on, this is no time for decent folk to be up and about,' Nana whispered. She ushered Ava back into her room and Ava climbed into bed. Nana sat on the side of her bed and tucked her in like she was a little child. The thought made Ava smile. It was quite nice being treated like that just for a moment.

'Why were you calling out for Corbie, Nana?' she asked.

'Because I'm an old fool,' Nana replied.

'But why Corbie?'

Nana sighed.

'In the old stories it was Corbie who led the crows, like I told you before. He lives in both worlds, our world and the spirit world, bridging the two. And I got muddled and thought the crows had started collecting my memories a bit early. My stories. They're meant to wait till we die, but ... well ... as I say, they've come for me early, maybe. Our souls are in our stories, little fragments in every one, and the crows keep them for us when we're gone. And I think that in my confusion I wanted Corbie to give them back, make my soul whole.'

'Could he do that? Could he give them back?'

She thought about Dustin's ritual.

We talk to the crows. They're like messengers to the dead. From the dead.

Nana shrugged. 'Who knows?' she asked. 'So much of the old lore is lost that it's hard to say for sure ... but, with a fair wind and the right person ... perhaps there are those who could do it ...'

Perhaps they could give Nana her memories back, Ava thought. Wouldn't it be lovely if that were true.

'What's he like, Corbie?' Ava asked.

'Oh, he's a dark one. Locals used to say he had one normal eye and one white eye. Others said that he only had one eye. The other was pecked out by a rival. Either way, he could see this life with his normal eye and the next life with whatever else he had left.'

Nana arched an eyebrow. Then she laughed. 'It could be that these are all just stories. Just silly old stories,' she said. 'But when you begin to lose them, like I am, losing my memories ... well, you realise that they're really quite valuable, those stories. Each one a little piece of your soul ... and there's nothing silly about them after all ...'

Nana went quiet. She withdrew into herself.

'Nana,' Ava whispered.

'Yes, Evelyn?' Nana replied faintly.

'It's Ava. Go to bed, Nana. Find Pop.'

Nana nodded absently. Then she shook herself and smiled and stood up.

'Yes, yes,' she said. 'Off to bed. This is no time for decent folk to be up and about.'

Ava dreamed of Corbie when she got back to sleep. The one-eyed crow chased her. Sometimes she chased him. Ghosts rose up all around and ran with him, spurred on, and he chattered away to them. 'Memories, memories for Corbie,' he called. 'Come, now, don't be shy.' Dad was there and Corbie spoke to him, too, though Ava could never quite get a good look at him as he flittered out of sight. Then she saw Nana walking lost and blind and with her soul trailing behind her in tatters like some kind of overgrown shadow, shedding bits of itself as she went, and Corbie flew through it all.

Eight

Robin was true to her word. She knocked for Ava the following morning and they walked up to St Francis' together. It was a nicer day with Robin by her side. The hallways buzzed with students as Ava and Robin walked towards their first class and Robin chatted away.

'I want to be a singer,' she said.

'Yeah?'

'Yeah.' Robin's eyes shone, excited. 'I've been writing songs for a couple of years now. Even had some singing lessons, though I was all right before. Sort of all right. Well, actually, the lessons helped. But still. I write all my own stuff.'

'I heard you singing last night,' Ava said. 'Do you ever do gigs? You know, with people watching and that?'

Robin took a deep breath. 'No, not yet,' she said. 'Just, you know, singing at home, in the yard ... sometimes into the mirror.' She looked at Ava and laughed. 'I use a hairbrush as a microphone and pretend like I'm singing to a whole room full of people, a whole stadium sometimes. I've got notebooks full of songs that I've written.

'But. Well, you know ...' Robin flushed. 'I've never had the courage to show them to anyone. Let alone sing to anyone. I've always been scared that people won't like them or that they'll think I'm not good enough.'

Ava just nodded.

'What do you reckon?' Robin asked.

'You've got a good voice,' Ava said. Then she blushed. 'You know, from what I heard yesterday. You can sing. So yeah. Why not? Go for it. I think you should. If you want to.'

Robin smiled.

Ava and Nana were sitting together in the living room later that evening. Pop had brought some flowers in from the garden, sweet peas freshly cut. He grew them in one straight line along one wall. 'Like my dad used to grow them during the war,' he liked to say. 'Everyone was digging for victory. There was no room for flowers.

Everything had to be vegetables or grazing, food to keep us going. But he always spared the smallest stretch along his allotment wall to grow sweet peas for my mum. Oh, she loved them. They brought the place to life.'

The smell filled every corner of the house. Nana sat next to them, sighed, disappeared into thought, and shook her head and looked at Ava.

'You know about her brother?' she asked.

'What?'

'The poor girl's brother. Her twin brother. Your mate, there.'

'Robin?'

'Yeah.'

'No.'

'Oh, well,' Nana said sadly. 'Poor thing.'

Nana fixed Ava with a stern eye.

'Jay. He died suddenly a couple of years back. Just a few months and then poor Jeanie and Phil were burying him. And he was such a lovely thing. Very gentle, very soft. Different to his sister in many ways. Not all ways, mind. You'd look at them and know they were brother and sister. Twins, even. Same expressions. Same way of speaking. But still different.

'And the strangest thing was that nobody was all too surprised when Jay got sick. And, mind, I can't remember him being sick a day in his life. But he was quiet in a way that Robin never was. As a little one, you'd hear her bawling night and day, running rings around Jeanie and Phil. I don't know how they coped. But he was so still, so calm. Ethereal, even. It was like he was never meant for this world. Like when he died he was returning to his rightful place. Even Jeanie said so, once.'

Ava had no idea how it could seem right for someone to die and no idea what ethereal meant either. Though, she thought, she did vaguely remember Mum telling her something a while back about Nana and Pop's neighbours, about the dead boy next door. Jay. She had shrugged it off at the time. It had meant nothing to her back then. Poor Robin, though, she thought. How on earth do you get over something like that? Then she thought about Dad. Yeah, she thought. How *do* you get over it?

Nana smiled to herself. 'Robin, that little thing, was full enough of life for a whole household,' she said. 'With Jay gone, she's full enough of life for them both. It doesn't make up for it. Not a bit, not even close. But it still warms my heart. Jeanie's and Phil's too, I daresay.'

Nana drifted as she spoke.

'She'll struggle to ever hear the crows,' she said softly. 'She's too full of life to hear them chattering on with their memories of death, of the dead. Yes she is . . .'

Nine

Robin came along with her later that week when Ava went to Dustin's ritual.

'You been to one before?' Ava asked.

'Yeah, a few,' Robin replied. She smiled ruefully. 'All of us misfits in school have been at one time or another. It beats doing nothing.'

They left school and headed up towards the woods. A group of people were clustered around the treeline. Robin picked a few out.

'That's Peter Morgan,' she said of a small, heavily browed boy. 'One of Dustin Marr's lackies. Hero worships him, it's so sad. Fancies him too, I reckon. And there's Sarah-Jane, Jackie . . . They're all right . . .' Jackie was near colourless. Her skin was pale and her hair was so fair that it was almost white. Sarah-Jane had fair skin, too, though her hair was red and curly, almost orange.

They got to the blackforest treeline and the others turned to look at them. Some scowled. Others looked at Ava and Robin blankly. Then something moved behind the trees. A scrawny and mean looking boy in torn trousers came out of the trees and looked them all over.

'Joe Walder,' Robin whispered to Ava.

'The crows are ready for you,' he told them.

Ava's heart skipped a beat.

They all filed in through the woods, up to where Dustin had been getting things ready. They headed along a slim woodland trail before leaving it to cut across through the bushes and undergrowth, eventually coming to a clearing.

Dustin greeted them there in silence. He looked like a statue, like the kind of marble statue you might see in a museum, gaunt and brooding as ever. He was standing in the middle of the clearing in a vest with a long and chunky necklace hanging over it. The necklace had what looked like a real crow's skull as a pendant. Other bones and a few black feathers were strung around the rest of it. His eyes burned as he looked them all over and Ava's own eyes burned as she met his gaze. She was the only one there to do so, though she felt herself blush a little.

A long and narrow hollow was cut deep into the clearing's floor. Thick fir branches had been placed over it to make a roof. A fire crackled inside. Nobody could see it from the outside, but a few wisps of smoke escaped through the fir branches. A large pile of stones stood at the edge of the clearing. It was shaped a bit like a pyramid, with lots of uneven stones stacked on top of each other.

'He calls it his cairn,' Robin whispered, nodding towards it. 'He carves names on it. The names of everyone who's ever taken part in the ritual.'

Dustin gestured and they all walked solemnly over to the pit. The others all sat in a circle around it and Ava took her cue from them, did as they did. Robin sat next to her.

Dustin walked around the outside of the circle. Anyone else might have looked ridiculous dressed as he was in vest and shorts with a necklace of bones around his neck. Ava would have laughed at them. Not Dustin Marr, though. Not there and then. He belonged in this world, a world of dark words and old magic. In one hand he held the crow's skull hanging from his necklace. He touched his other hand palm down on each of their heads in turn as he went, as though blessing them.

'You have come for the crows, to hear their stories, to listen to fragments of lost souls long since dead,' he said. 'Their words are not for everyone. And those they choose must submit to them or else be struck down dead. Do you all agree to the crows' terms?'

They all mumbled and nodded.

'Yes,' Ava whispered under her breath.

Dustin walked behind her and touched his sooty palm to the top of her head. She shuddered and her heart beat so hard that she thought it was going to jump out of her chest. But he moved on. He touched his hand to Robin's head, then he came to Peter Morgan, who shrank away, squealing as Dustin lay his hand on his head.

'You have been chosen,' he said.

Peter Morgan was white and shaking and his eyes were wide with fright, but nobody ever said no to Dustin, not here.

'Do you wish to hear what the crows have to tell you?' Dustin asked.

'Yes, I . . . I do,' Peter Morgan stuttered.

'Do you swear to listen or else be struck down?'

'I do.'

'Into the flames with you, then.'

Peter Morgan climbed down into the hollow as Dustin held a couple of branches aside. Smoke billowed up. It got into Ava's nose and into her eyes, stinging and choking. She only barely held back a coughing fit, but she was determined not to show weakness in front of this lot.

Peter Morgan was curling up into a ball in the hollow the last they saw of him. Smoke surrounded him. The fire was at the far end. Dustin fished in his pocket and pulled out what looked like little bones, and he threw them into the flames before putting the branches back in place and covering up the hollow. Ava heard the flames pop and hiss, crackling around the bones.

Dustin began to chant.

'Corbie, corvus, corvie. Corbie, corvus, corvie.'

They all chanted along with him.

'Corbie, corvus, corvie. Corbie, corvus, corvie.'

Then Dustin drew his finger across his throat and they all fell silent. They got up and walked away to the edge of the clearing. Nobody was allowed to speak from then until Peter Morgan emerged. Nobody needed to tell

Ava. The silence was heavy and thick and right then she couldn't imagine ever breaking it.

Dustin took out a sharp piece of flint as they all waited and began to scratch lines into the cairn. Ava watched him. The lines were brittle and hard and reminded her of the runes he had carved into his staff.

PETER MORGAN, he wrote.

'Sometimes the ritual is over quickly,' Robin had told her beforehand. Whoever it was would come out shaken. 'Sometimes it takes a little longer, though,' she had said. 'They stagger out covered in ash and soot, shaking all over.'

Peter Morgan took a long time. They waited and waited for him. Five minutes and then maybe ten. They began to look at each other nervously. Nobody spoke. Dustin wouldn't allow it. But they all knew what each other were thinking.

What if one day somebody didn't come out?

'You bring him out before he's done with the crows and he will have to choose death,' Dustin growled as he sensed their unrest. 'The crows will steal his wits, his soul ... a death of the soul, and there's nothing worse than that.'

But where the others were growing nervous, Ava began to get a bit bored with the waiting. She had expected more than this of Dustin, more of his ritual. She glared around at the others, but they were all still silent, staring at the hollow. *It's all rubbish, isn't it?* she thought. It had been silly of her to take Nana's stories seriously. Dustin's too. There was no talking to crows. No listening out for lost souls' stories.

The smoke still poured from the ground. It stung her eyes some more. Wingbeats sounded from above and she looked up, but she couldn't see anything through all that smoke and the evening's gloaming. Birds called out. *Caw, caw,* the crow's call. Then her vision swam for a second. Her head grew a little light.

She heard the crows. She heard a voice, a man's voice, low and deep and rumbling. A faint laugh lay behind it all. She imagined Dad for the briefest second. Then a boy's voice came, young sounding but cackling lightly like an old man. *We can give you what you want,* it said. But it was gone as quickly as it had come and she blinked and cursed herself.

Don't be so silly, she thought. She sighed. *It's just a stupid game,* she told herself.

Isn't it?

She wasn't so sure. Not right then.

And then, at last, a couple of branches twitched over the hollow. A soot black hand came out, then another. Both hands gripped the ground and pulled and Peter came out, dark grey with ash, with only the whites of his eyes showing. He heaved and choked and spluttered, shaking all over. Then he made himself stand straight and look at Dustin.

'The crows spoke to me,' he wheezed, and Ava knew instantly that he was lying.

Ten

Ava heard the voice from the ritual in her dreams that night. It called to her, deep and rumbling. Then she was woken abruptly in the early hours of the morning. It was still dark outside and at first she didn't know what had woken her. Then she heard footsteps and somebody whispering loudly.

'Corbie, you old tease! Where did you go?'

'Nana!'

She got out of bed. Nana was fumbling along the landing again and calling out for Corbie.

'Nana!'

Nana started and looked at her, confused for a second. Then understanding dawned.

'Oh dear,' she sighed. 'Oh, my dear. Look at me, at it again.'

'Come on, Nana,' Ava said. 'Come on. Let's get you back to bed.'

Nana looked none the worse for wear for her midnight rambling the following morning.

'You know, it's nearly Beltane,' she said.

'What's that?' Ava asked.

'It's one of her festivals,' Pop said with a rueful smile. 'Old pagan that she is. The first day of summer for many.'

'Walpurgisnacht in Germany, the festival of flowers in Ancient Rome,' Nana muttered, nodding to herself as she remembered. 'When we'd crown the May Queen and recognise life in its fullest.'

Ava thought of her dad. Life in its fullest? What a load of rubbish. Life wasn't full. It was short and brutal and pointless in the end.

'For me it's May Day,' Pop said with a big grin. 'First of May. International Workers' Day, when we'd stick it to our bosses and the government and all that. The unions would all celebrate. A day for power in ordinary folks' hands.'

'That and more,' Nana said. She smiled at Ava.

Mum sighed behind her and shook her head.

'It's always the same,' she told Ava. 'One on about magic and fairy tales. The other on about industrial action, workers' rights . . .'

'But the industrial world will always fail us. Only nature is true . . .' Nana replied.

Pop snorted.

'It doesn't put food on the table though, does it? All that mumbo jumbo!'

'It does,' Nana said. 'A cornucopia. Food for our bellies and for our souls, and more besides.'

They grinned at each other, winding each other up, and Mum sighed and shook her head once more.

Robin knocked for Ava after breakfast. It was a warm enough day and she wore a short skirt and T-shirt, bright trainers, all colourful. They walked up through the fields and along the treeline. Crows rose up from the trees, circling up above, calling to one another. Ava fancied they called down to her. Memories of the dead. Something occurred to Ava.

'Why do you go to the rituals?' she asked Robin.

'Oh, you know . . .' Robin replied, vague.

'They bring us memories of the dead,' Ava said quietly.

Robin paused for a second. Then she nodded.

'Your brother. Jay.'

Robin nodded again.

'Nana told me about it, though I remember my mum telling me about it a couple of years ago. You know. When it happened,' Ava said in a quiet voice. 'I'm sorry.'

Robin shrugged.

'It's like your dad,' she said. 'And I bet people tell you they're sorry about it. And it doesn't really mean anything, does it?'

'No. No it doesn't. But I'm sorry for not thinking before.'

Robin shrugged and nodded. 'I've never really met anyone else who's lost someone. Grandparents, yeah. But not someone younger, someone ... you know ... someone who should have had more time. I've not met many people, to be honest. I haven't had any proper friends since Jay died, cos I don't always get people.'

Ava nodded. She understood.

'I worry about him,' Robin carried on. 'I worry about wherever he is.'

'He's probably in the same place as my dad,' Ava whispered.

'Probably, wherever that is ... if there even is anywhere ...' Robin narrowed her eyes. 'And I've sometimes wondered about talking to him. You know, through the ritual. But... well, it's all nonsense, I reckon.'

'Yeah?'

'Yeah. Jay isn't in a stupid hole in the ground, talking to stupid birds and stupid Dustin Marr.'

'You don't think so?'

'Of course I don't.'

Ava nodded and they carried on walking through the sunshine together.

Eleven

The blackforest was tranquil in those late spring evenings. Or parts of it were at least, on the edges. The sunlight dipped to the horizon and its light danced over briar and bramble. Bugs buzzed in the air and leaves rustled underfoot. It was all cool and peaceful.

There was a spot far from the ritual site, an open part with a crude firepit in the middle surrounded by stones.

'We go there sometimes,' Robin told Ava. 'You know, just to hang out.'

It was no day for a ritual and there were people there who would never come to it. They would never be invited. They got a fire going, a great bonfire that some of the boys from the year above spent the evening feeding with big sticks and small logs. It was just wood and leaves, no magic, no darkness. Ava and Robin sat together, apart from the rest. The flames burned fierce as evening fell and the blackforest submitted to night.

Dustin was there, also sitting apart from the rest. The flames danced in his eyes. The shadows clung to that marble skin.

Luke Jenkins sat nearby with his guitar. He was in the year above Ava and Robin and loads of girls fancied him. He always sat around with his guitar, with longish curls falling around his face, and all the girls simpered. Ava couldn't see what the fuss was about. The simpering annoyed her. Luke was a poser, and he didn't have much to pose about, from what she could tell. A few girls sat around him then as he played and Ava shook her head. Dustin shook his head, too. He glared at Luke and the flames seemed to dim down a little.

Luke finished a song. He looked up and caught Dustin glaring. Dustin took a long pull from a bottle and Luke laughed.

'Drowning his sorrows just like his dad,' he said.

The clearing fell quiet. The flames shimmered across Dustin's bottle. A lonely crow called out from deep within the blackforest and Ava held her breath.

Dustin stood up tall and gaunt. The fire burned lower still as he looked at Luke without blinking. Luke put his guitar down and stood and took a step back, suddenly unsure of himself. The girls around him edged away a little.

Dustin took a step forwards. He looked around, his face almost feral as people avoided his gaze. Only Ava kept looking. Their eyes met and her ears roared. She shook her head ever so slightly as Dustin looked at her. *Don't do anything stupid.* She willed it.

Dustin smiled at her and his smile was more terrifying than anything, like he was baring his teeth at her. Then he laughed. It was a brutal sound. Then he picked up his bottle and turned his back on the fire. The blackforest's gloom thickened outside the clearing as he strode towards it without looking back. The shadows swallowed him whole. The trees swallowed him. Far off, the crows chattered and laughed.

'What did Luke mean about Dustin's dad?' Ava asked Robin as they walked home a little later.

'You know,' Robin said. She shrugged. 'He likes his drink, Danny Marr. Likes it a lot.'

Twelve

Ava saw it for herself a few days later. She and Pop were on their way back from the chippy round the corner. The sun wasn't long set and it cast a ruddy glow across the horizon. Darkness above it all and red light below. A couple of crows flew down and glared at them from a nearby fence. Their glossy feathers shimmered under the streetlight's glare as they turned to glower at Ava and Pop with an unsettling intensity. They hopped closer with their beady eyes fixed on Ava and Pop as if sizing them up. A shiver ran down Ava's spine as they cawed harshly, shattering the night's peace.

'Oh dear,' Pop said, not seeming to notice them.

'What?'

'Look.'

He nodded towards the end of the street. A shape shambled along it, swaying through the darkness with each footstep.

'Danny Marr,' Pop said in a low voice. He sounded sad as he said it. Danny Marr emerged from the shadows, bulky and unkempt. He took a deep breath and muttered something to himself. Then he shouted.

'Come on, you waste of space!'

Dustin hurried around the corner, caught up with his dad, and put an arm around his shoulders to steady him. His dad collapsed slightly into him.

'I'm sorry, I didn't mean it,' his dad said. 'You're not a waste of space. You're a beauty. A beautiful thing in an ugly world.'

'OK, Dad,' Dustin said. He heaved and managed to get his dad walking again.

'Beautiful like your mother when all else is gone to hell,' Danny Marr carried on. 'Who remembers the last time any of us laughed?'

'I don't know, Dad,' Dustin said.

'I know you don't. You've got no brains. None of us do, not any more.'

Dustin's dad looked up and glared at Pop across the

street. Lamplight hit him and Ava saw just how much he looked like his son, all heavy brows, all scowls, but with none of Dustin's beauty.

'None of us do,' he repeated. 'Not even you, Tommy Shepherd!'

'OK, Danny,' Pop said. 'Get yourself home, now. And be kinder to that son of yours.'

Dustin looked embarrassed. It didn't suit him, Ava thought. She was so used to seeing him self-assured and in control but now he just stared at his feet. His dad looked furious. He swore.

'Who are you to tell me what to do?' he demanded.

'An old friend,' Pop replied. 'If you've got any left in the world.'

'Bah!'

Danny Marr limped off down the street and disappeared into the night. Dustin glared at Ava before hurrying off after his dad and Ava's heart went out to him. Pop sighed. 'You've got to be made of stern stuff to put up with nonsense like that every day and still go out and face the world,' he said. 'The poor boy.'

They carried on for a bit.

'Your nana used to babysit Dustin Marr,' he said. Ava

nodded. She knew. They had told her. 'She loved that boy and she loved his mother, Eileen. She was from a good family and back then Danny had a decent job. There were plenty of good jobs round here. But he drank even back then. He drank and he was violent and your nana wasn't safe there after a while. That was, what, eight years ago? Before the works up in Headington closed down and put everyone not already on their pension out of a job, Danny included. I begged her to stop, though it broke her heart to walk away from the family. From Dustin and Eileen.'

Ava lay in bed that night, replaying the scene in her mind. The embarrassment Dustin had clearly felt was still fresh. She took a deep breath and decided to talk to Dustin about it when she next had a chance. She would offer to help. She had no idea what kind of help she could give, but she had to do something.

A crow swooped down towards her window as she thought it through. Its wings cut through the moonlight before it landed on her windowsill with an ominous thud. It perched there, unmoving, with dark eyes gleaming, as she opened the curtain to see what was going on. It stood there watching her with an unblinking and predatory stillness.

'Go away,' she whispered. 'Just . . . just go away . . .'

She didn't manage much sleep that night, worrying about Dustin. Then Dustin put another ritual on before she had a chance to speak to him. Ava tried to catch him in the corridor at one point, but he pushed past her, refusing to look at her. Then Joe Walder came up to her and Robin at break, skinny and scruffy and mean looking as ever.

'Tonight,' he said. 'Usual time, usual place.' And that was that.

Thirteen

They all met up and headed into the woods as before and found the same spot. The greenery and the rucked earth. The entrance to another world. Small plumes of smoke were already beginning to rise through the fir branches.

Dustin stood by his cairn, watching them all with his arms crossed. He was wearing the same necklace and vest as before. The same shorts. There was no baseball cap today. His ragged hair was swept back behind his ears and there was soot smudged in places over his face and neck. This time he also carried his little staff, finished now, the carved skull gleaming with fresh polish.

He smirked when he saw Ava.

They all took their places as before, sitting around the hollow. The smoke grew thicker. Ava could hear the fire crackling below as Dustin began to circle around behind them. She looked at the others, all these locals from Crawford, from where the crows made their home by the water. She wondered how many of them had gone into that hollow, breathed the smoke, shut their eyes and listened. How many had heard anything at all?

None of them, she thought. Not a single one of them.

'You have come for the crows, to hear what they have to say,' Dustin told them. He walked around touching their heads one by one. 'But the crows' words aren't for everyone,' he carried on. 'They have powerful memories, memories of those who came before us. They only choose who they choose. And who they choose must submit to them or be struck down dead. Do you all agree to the crows' terms?'

'Yes,' Ava said out loud. She thought of Nana and Corbie and she nodded. She thought of her dad, kept from her in death, and she thought about the sensation she had felt at the first ritual, the dreams she had had afterwards, the voices she had heard. She thought about the crows following her and Pop and the one that had come once more to her window and she shivered, though she stayed firm.

'Yes,' she whispered.

Dustin walked behind her and put his hand on her head. He kept it there and squeezed a little too tightly with his fingertips pressing into her scalp. She shuddered and her heart began to beat so hard that she thought it was going to jump out of her chest.

'The crows bring us close to the dead. You have been chosen,' he told her. 'Do you wish to hear what they have to tell you?'

'Yes,' she said.

'Do you swear to listen or else be struck down?'

'I do.'

'Into the flames with you, then.'

The hollow was cramped and dirty. Dustin held a couple of branches aside and she climbed in. She slid down the last little bit as some of the dry earth gave out from beneath her. She gasped as she got to the bottom and the momentum carried her on. The heat blasted her, crackled all around. Her lungs burned as she breathed in the scalding air.

This is what it must be like to be burned alive, she thought.

She thought of her dad's funeral. They had burned him too, until he was nothing but ashes. Mum still had the ashes in an urn at home. Ava sometimes heard her talking to them, though Mum didn't know.

People chanted above.

'Corbie, corvus, corvie. Corbie, corvus, corvie.'

Ava's head swam in the heat. Her eyes stung. Tears gathered in her lashes and she squinted as everything went fuzzy. She was struggling to breathe in the heat. Her lungs were heavy. She found herself lying curled up in a ball as the chanting carried on.

'Corbie, corvus, corvie. Corbie, corvus, corvie.'

Then all fell silent except for the fire's crackling. Ava tried to blink her eyes open. In the brief glimpses she managed, she saw a little bird skull in the fire. The remains of burned feathers lay about next to the fire alongside a couple more bones here and there.

The skull moved. It rocked in the heat. It seemed to Ava to turn and face her. Heat washed over her so that she was close to fainting from it. The chattering of birds and the flapping of distant wings mixed in with the fire's popping and crackling. She blinked her eyes open once more and saw the bird's skull looking at her. Other bones had joined with it and burning feathers had given it a plumage so that it seemed to stand there, a full bird made of flame.

Corbie, corvus, corvie, the fire croaked, and everything went dark.

Fourteen

She climbed out of the hollow. Everything was cold and dark and she felt clear-headed and calm for the first time in a long time. Everyone was gone. The air tasted different. Outlines were blurred for a second before focussing. It might have looked like the clearing but it was not. It was somewhere else entirely, a different world.

Birds flew overhead. Black shapes swirled. The crows descended and began to land in a wide circle all around her. They were death's guide, carrion birds, takers of stories, and Ava wondered briefly if she was dead, if this was the end of her story.

No, no, she thought. She could feel it. She was alive, if a little disconnected.

Disconnected from what?

She looked at the woods and the shadows between the trees grew darker.

Disconnected from it all. Not dead, but halfway there, perhaps. She began to shiver as more and more dark shapes landed. A murder of crows, she thought. Fifty or more of them stood in a ring around her.

Foolish child, the crows seemed to whisper. She heard their voices in her head.

We have nothing to do with murder, with death. It is around you whom death hangs like a shroud, blanketing all.

'What do you want with me?' Ava asked.

They all turned their heads as one, watching her side-on, each through one eye.

Nothing, fool. It was you who sought us out. What do you want with us?

She was scared. Terrified. Her legs shook and her breath caught in her throat as she looked at them all standing there, eyeing her.

What do you want with us?

She gasped and spoke, spoke without really thinking.

'I want you to give my nana her memories back.'

Ha ha ha ha ha ha. The crows cackled and cawed.

Something rustled in the trees. A single crow flew out from amidst the branches, from beneath the canopy. It had a few white feathers in its wings and a fierce light in one of its eyes. The other eye socket was empty. It landed before Ava and scowled, hopped closer, croaked. The rest all fell silent.

Fool child, it whispered.

Corbie.

Shadows clung to Corbie for a moment, then unfolded, uncoiled, grew, and where before a crow with white feathers in its wings had stood, now stood a boy who looked like he was a few years younger than Ava. Except that he wasn't. He was clearly ancient, an ancient thing taking on the guise of a young boy. His one good eye was dark and his skin was pale, so much like Ava's own. His hair was as dark as Ava's, though it had flashes of white at the front, two long white locks meeting at his forehead. He seemed dusty to Ava, somehow. He was dressed simply in long, ragged robes of dark grey and black which reminded her of cobwebs in the darkness.

Fool.

Corbie stepped closer to Ava.

'Do you really think it's possible to get your nana's

memories back?' he asked. His voice was an old man's, thin and reedy.

Ava continued to shake. She was terrified. Corbie knew it, too. He took a step towards Ava, smiling like a predator toying with her from just a few paces away.

'Well?' he asked. Then he shrieked. 'TELL ME!'

Ava jumped, stumbled backwards, half fell over in her fear.

'Do you really think it's possible?' Corbie hissed. 'Do you?'

'Yes!'

Corbie stopped, suddenly still as a statue. He smiled.

'Yes?'

Ava nodded frantically. She was already nodding before she realised that she had spoken the truth.

'Yes,' she said again. Her throat was tight and it was hard to get the words out. 'Yes. I do. I do believe it.' It has to be true, she thought. I can't lose Nana too, not as well as Dad, not like this with her fading away, her soul being pecked apart. She imagined it then, saw it clearly. Nana's soul was being pecked to pieces and she was disappearing.

It was too much.

The crows burst into laughter once more, cackling at her, but Corbie was quiet.

'Well then,' he whispered. He took a step towards Ava and the cackling died down. All was calm suddenly, though Ava was still tense.

Corbie nodded.

'Your nana's stories are delicious,' he said quietly. 'By far some of the best. The stories . . . so rich.'

'So . . . so it's true?' Ava stammered. Her eyes burned. She curled her hands into fists and anger found its way through the fear. They had indeed been stealing her nana's memories . . .

'You said it was true,' Corbie said simply. 'You believe we can give them back. That means we took them in the first place, no? You know. We know. Yes, it's true. Her memories are the sweetest nectar to us. But to you, to your world . . .' He sneered and spat on the ground in front of her. 'Nobody in your world listens to them, nobody pays them any heed. It's all machines and worse, no place for the old stories. They have no room in your world. So why wouldn't we take them?'

'But she's not dead . . . you're meant to guide the dead and take their memories, aren't you?'

Corbie cackled once more in his old man's voice.

'Soul death,' he whispered. 'If you don't heed us then you will be soul dead. Your world heeds nothing. Not us, not anything of our world, not any more. So we name you soul dead and we take what we will. Your nana first because she is closest to us and her stories are so sweet. But she will not be the last.'

'What can I do?' Ava asked. She didn't understand, not fully. But if there was a way that she could get them to return Nana's memories then she had to know. She had to do it.

'Do?' Corbie asked. He began to walk a slow circle around Ava. Ava turned on the spot with him, keeping the strange little boy in her eyes. Hundreds of eyes watched them from that wide ring of crows. Corbie smiled after a little while.

'A soul for a soul . . .' he whispered.

'What?' Ava asked.

'A soul for a soul.'

'I don't understand.'

'Because you're a fool. But think on it. Think. We will come for you when the time is right.'

Corbie stopped walking and suddenly a crow stood

before Ava once more, jet black feathers with just a few flashes of white in his wings. He cawed and his eyes burned and heat washed over Ava and she woke up in the hollow in the ground with the fire right before her. Smoke curled all around her and she coughed and spluttered. Her blood ran cold even as her skin began to burn. Ash clung to everything and she choked on the hot air. Hurrying, she pushed herself backwards, away from the fire, scrambled up the hollow's side, and frantically shoved her way through the branches.

The first gasp of fresh, cool evening air was just about the sweetest thing she had ever tasted. She heaved herself up over the hollow's edge and lay on the ground, panting. A shadow fell over her and she thought once more of the crows circling. She looked up, though, and saw Dustin glaring down at her. His eyes met hers and he reached out a hand. She took it and he hauled her to her feet.

'Tell me you saw them,' he growled. 'Tell me you heard them.'

'I did,' she whispered. 'I did.'

She looked over Dustin's shoulder and saw her name carved into the cairn.

AVA BRIDGER.

Fifteen

Ava stumbled over to Robin, who opened her arms and held onto her. The ash that covered Ava's front smeared onto her, but she didn't care. She just held onto Ava.

'I don't think anyone's ever been down there that long,' she whispered.

They left the others. Robin led her back through the woods as everyone watched in silence. Nobody came over to Ava to ask her what she had seen. Only Dustin seemed content. Only he seemed happy.

'Ava, seriously, are you OK?' Robin asked as they reached the edge of the trees. Ava had barely said two words, but what could she say? She had no words. She had no way of understanding what on earth had just happened.

A soul for a soul.

She took a deep breath.

'Yeah, I'm OK,' she lied. 'It's all OK.'

'I've never seen Dustin look like that before,' Robin said. 'He's usually kind of intense, but that was something else.'

Ava turned and looked back up at the woods. She saw a murder of crows taking flight. She heard their wings beating. She heard rustling, voices, whispering. For a moment she even thought that she heard laughter as they wheeled around the forest's canopy before diving back down into its clutches. The shadows between the trees moved. Some got darker and she was sure there was something in there looking out at her.

'Can you hear that?' she asked quietly.

'What?'

Robin looked spooked. Ava just shook her head. It was all too much. It was all too strange.

'Come on,' Robin said. 'Let's get you home.'

A cold breeze cut through the night. They huddled down into their jackets as they walked and Ava ended up telling Robin everything. It all came spilling out of her. She told her about the crow skull sort of coming to life, about blacking out and the crows talking to her, about Corbie and what he had said to her.

'You think I'm nuts.'

Robin nodded. 'I do,' she said. 'But I think everyone's nuts. Why would you be special?'

'Do you believe me?'

'I don't think you would lie.'

They carried on walking. 'I still don't believe the others,' Robin said after a bit. 'They're all faking it. You can see it. I reckon Dustin can see it, too. He's always disappointed. That's how he looks, even if he does keep managing to hoodwink people into playing his stupid game. But with you . . . something was different.'

'I know.'

'I'd be nervous of that one if I were you.'

'Dustin?'

'Yeah.'

'Yeah,' Ava said. 'I know.'

'Do you reckon you'll go back?'

'Maybe,' Ava said. 'I'm not sure. Just . . . maybe.'

Those cryptic words. *Think on it. Think. We will come for you when the time is right.*

'I think I might have to,' she said quietly.

'You all right, love?' Mum asked when she saw her. 'You look white as a sheet. And what's that you're covered in? And that smell! Is that smoke?'

Ava shook her head. 'There was an old campfire up in the woods,' she said. 'I tripped, fell into it. I'll be fine after a shower.'

'Yeah, well, if you say so,' Mum said. She was frowning. 'Go and get yourself cleaned up before dinner.'

Nana was standing in her bedroom doorway. She stared as Ava passed her on her way to her own room. She smiled vacantly, but something gleamed in her eyes.

'Corbie got you,' she whispered.

Sixteen

'Sod this place,' Dustin said.

Ava nodded. She looked up at St Francis' and agreed. Sod this place.

'Let's not bother today,' she said. She wanted a break from it all. Plus, she was quite happy for the chance to spend some time alone with Dustin, wary of him though she was.

'I know just the place to go,' Dustin told her.

'Yeah?'

'Yeah, I want to show you something.'

So they turned on their heels as everyone else streamed in through the school gates for the morning bell and headed off, through alleys and winding backstreets.

'Where're we going?' she asked, but Dustin didn't

answer. A couple of crows wheeled overhead as they went. A couple more followed behind, perching on fences and tree limbs, watching.

We'll come for you soon enough.

Ava shivered.

They came to a small cottage on the outskirts of town after a short walk. It looked like it had once been a nice place, though now it was shabby and rundown, with mouldy, cracked wooden window frames and weeds choking the garden. It looked half abandoned.

'What's that?' Ava asked.

'My place,' Dustin said. He set his chin and glowered at her, defiant. She just nodded.

They didn't go to the cottage, though. Fields opened up behind it and a large barn stood a little way off which had definitely seen better days. The whole thing was dilapidated, with holes in the walls, chunks of roof missing, and filth everywhere. It was exactly where Dustin seemed to be leading her.

'Come on,' he said.

'In there?'

He nodded. 'Yeah.'

'Is it safe?'

'Probably not. But who cares? I spend loads of time in there and I'm OK.'

The air was filled with the earthy scent of hay and bird excrement and the faint rustling of feathers as they approached the barn. Its windows were all smashed and shattered. Ava saw a black shape move behind one, then another, and her breath caught in her throat. Shadows danced within and the thought of them made Ava's skin prickle.

The crows.

Half-light swallowed them as Dustin led her into the barn. The smell of excrement grew stronger and the sound of feathers rustling grew immediately louder.

It was massive. The high ceiling opened up to the heavens in several places, letting in light that played across dust and debris. Upright wooden beams rose from the earth like pillars and held everything solid. Like Dustin's cairn, Ava found herself thinking as she saw a particularly stout though partly broken one.

Everything was smeared with greasy bird poo. Feathers lay everywhere, piled high in dust and dirt, and Ava wrinkled her nose. A couple of crows flew overhead, from one end of the barn to the other. Eyes burned from dark corners, all watching her and Dustin. There were dozens of them.

A few overturned crates sat just in front of a raised platform at the end. Dustin folded himself down onto one. He nodded at another and Ava crossed over to it and sat down. Dead birds littered the floor. Plenty of bird bones lay around about, hidden in the corners, in all that dust and clutter.

'It's where you get your bones for the ritual, for your necklace,' she said.

Dustin nodded. 'Yeah. You saw where I live. It's horrible. And worse, it's got my dad in it. So I spend as much time as I can out here, even in winter when it's freezing. I thought the crows would chase me away at first, but they didn't. They just watch me, let me take their bones. I don't think they're sentimental. They don't care about their dead, about the bones. I can take what I want.'

'That's a bit . . .'

'What?'

'I don't know,' Ava said. Disgusting, she thought. 'Grisly,' she said.

'You take part in the ritual,' Dustin replied simply. That was the end of it. He was right. He took the bones to conduct the ritual with. By taking part in the ritual, she used them too. If he was grisly then so was she. If he was disgusting . . . well, so was she. So were all the others.

A crow cawed high up in the rafters. Then another and another. They made her flinch, but she took a deep breath to steady herself. She stood up and began to root around, kicking at the dust and feathers. She uncovered plenty more bones. Scared as she was, she wouldn't be a hypocrite, not now that Dustin had pointed it out. If she was going to use the bones in the ritual then she could at least look into them a bit more, maybe even choose some.

'These,' she said.

She held her breath, steeled herself, and picked up a handful of bones. Some were sticky. The tissue around them wasn't fully decomposed. Her stomach lurched but she wouldn't ever show it, especially not to Dustin. She put them on the table.

'These, for the next ritual,' she said.

Dustin looked at them and nodded. He opened his school bag and swept them in.

'They'll need cleaning,' he said. 'I'll take care of it.'

He glared at her.

'How did you pick them?' he asked. 'Those ones?'

'I don't know,' she said. 'Just random.'

'Random . . . right.'

'What?'

A crow swept down from high up in the rafters and Ava flinched again. It landed in front of the overturned crates and glared at Dustin. Then it turned and held Ava in its eyes and squawked and jumped towards her.

Those bones are good, it seemed to say as it swooped past. *Use them well.*

'So what is it?' Dustin asked.

'What?' Ava asked. She sat down and stared dead ahead, realising how tense she must look. She could feel Dustin watching her.

'Why are you suddenly scared of them?'

'I'm not.'

'You are. Don't lie to me.'

She shook her head and tried to relax.

'I was always scared of them.'

'Stop lying to me.'

She was silent.

'The ritual worked where it's never worked before,' Dustin said quietly. 'No matter how hard I tried . . . What is it that's so special about you, Ava Bridger?'

She shrugged.

'Nothing,' she said.

'Don't pretend. I saw it the first time I ever saw you. Then the ritual worked, out of nowhere.'

'I don't know. But I didn't try. I just . . . I don't know. It just happened for me. And I wish it hadn't.'

'What?' Dustin sounded angry now. 'How could you say something like that?'

A chorus rang around them as crows screeched and cawed.

'You weren't there, didn't see what I saw—'

'I know!' Dustin shouted. He jumped to his feet and walked around in front of her.

'I know I didn't see it. I've never seen it, no matter how hard I've worked at it. And now you do it with no bother, and you're saying you wish you'd never. How dare you?'

She stood. The fear and the anger were too much. She glared at him and felt her heart racing.

'Because it was terrifying,' she shouted back. 'They were terrifying. Do you have any idea what kind of creatures they are, how they can make you feel?'

'No. You know I don't.'

She turned her back on him and gazed up at the rafters.

'They're horrible, evil,' she said. The crows chattered away, laughing once more.

'They're not evil,' Dustin said. 'Only humans talk about good and evil. They just are what they are.'

'And what they are is awful.'

'So that's it? You're giving up? Not going to go back for more because what, you're afraid?'

'No,' she said quietly. 'I want to do it again. I need to, and soon.'

'Why?'

'Because they told me so. Or they said they'll come for me, at least. I don't know, but they need something from me, and I need something from them. So I'm stuck. I don't have a choice, do I? I need to go back in.'

'So you need me, you need them, they need you ...' He scowled at the crows. 'I need them, too. But they've never cared about that ...' Dustin sighed and shook his head and plonked himself back down onto his crate. He nodded at her crate, telling her to do the same.

'I'm going to get away from here,' he said. 'I'm going to fly away. Go wild, go live in the wild. So yeah, I'll help you. But it'll have to be soon, Ava Bridger, because I don't plan to stick around here much longer. Your nana showed me that much.'

'What do you mean?'

'All the stories she told me when I was younger. The stories she told me and my mum. Everything is about the wild, about nature. That's where true life is, she used to say. A better life, or at least a more honest one. And that's where I want to go. Away from here to somewhere better and more honest.'

They hung out for a bit. Sometimes they chatted. Mostly Dustin just kept his thoughts to himself. Crows came and went, hunting, feeding, and they both sat and watched them for an hour or more. Then their reverie was broken as a shout rose from outside the barn. It was a thick voice, clearly angry, cursing and screaming. Dustin froze. Then he swore and jumped up.

'Come on,' he said. He threw his bag over his shoulder and jogged over to the far end of the barn, opposite where they had come in, as far as possible from that shouting. Ava followed him and they ducked through a smaller opening in the barn's wall. A patch of woodland stood a few hundred yards off and Dustin led her to it as the shouting got louder.

Danny Marr rushed into view around the edge of the barn. He saw them and shouted even louder.

'You, boy! You been in there again? Heathens, both of you, all of you! Heathens!'

He bellowed some more but Ava and Dustin got to the treeline and disappeared into the woods. Dustin didn't say another word to her that afternoon, not one more thing.

Seventeen

They were beginning to lose Nana more and more. She would disappear from them like she had that time when they had gone out walking. Her eyes would go dull and lifeless and faraway, solemn and all too often sad.

'Oh, Evelyn,' she would sigh if she ever looked at Ava when she was like it. On her worst days, though, she wouldn't even do that. It was like Ava wasn't there, like Nana couldn't see her at all. Then it seemed to Ava like Nana was hollow. They would be sitting together and suddenly she would fade out completely like she had been emptied.

Pop's eyes were often rimmed with red. Mum said he wasn't sleeping properly.

'Love, love,' he would whisper to Nana. He would hold

her hand in his. Sometimes she would stroke his arm absently. Other times she wouldn't notice him. At those times you could lift her hand and drop it, and it would fall straight down like a dead weight. Her soul was being eaten up and only a few ragged fragments remained, Ava thought. Each time was worse, like she came back with less and less of herself.

'Love,' Pop would whisper.

Then she would return to them. She would smile slyly and maybe blush and Pop would look like his life had been on pause and somebody had just pressed the play button, starting it back up again. 'Where've you been, love?' he would ask.

'Off, just off,' she would reply.

Pop would smile and try not to look scared. He tried not to look scared for Nana's sake and for Ava's, though Ava knew. Nana knew too, most likely, when she was in her right mind. He was gentle with her. Mum and Ava both struggled to be patient and struggled not to take it to heart. But Pop was all tenderness.

Nana was on the front step when Ava got home from school one day. Mum was out at work, her first day at her new job. The sun was still casting a rosy glow over everything. Ava sat down next to Nana and leaned her head against her shoulder.

'My poor old head is like a colander,' Nana said. 'All holes, with all my memories and thoughts leaking out.'

'How can we plug the holes up?' Ava asked quietly.

'Oh, love,' Nana said. 'I don't think that's going to happen. Besides, enough's already gone that I think we'd be too late. You know, I can't even remember how to tie my shoelaces? Imagine that, eh?'

'What does it feel like?' Ava asked.

'Oh, my love, it's not nice.' Nana sighed. 'It's like disappearing from your own self for a few minutes. Longer, sometimes. Often, actually. You've seen me. I float away and can't see anything except what's right in front of me. And without your memories, what's in front of you doesn't mean all that much. It's so foolish . . .'

'It's not foolish,' Ava said, but Nana wasn't really listening.

'Imagine my thoughts are like grains of wheat or barley that you throw to the birds,' she whispered. 'Each one different. And the birds mess them up, and fly off with them until there's no getting them back and no sorting out one from the other . . .'

Ava glared out of her window when she went to bed that evening and saw the crows in the garden. They've come for her, she thought. They're taking more and more, faster and faster. They watched her back, greedy, beady little eyes shimmering.

They'd come for her.

Eighteen

Life wasn't all doom and gloom. The sunshine had been near enough constant. Robin, too, had been constant ever since Ava had moved here. Ava was sitting in the back yard with Nana the following afternoon when Robin came out into her own back yard. She smiled over the fence at them.

'Hello, Miriam,' she said.

'Oh, goodness me,' Nana said. She looked surprised, though she recovered quickly. 'Hello . . . Yes, hello, love.'

'It's Robin, Miriam. But it doesn't matter.'

'Robin. Well then. Yes, I do remember. Silly old biddy.' Nana smiled at Robin. 'I'm too old and foolish by half, and too tired with it. I think I shall head in and rest my weary bones before dinner.'

So saying, she headed back indoors, tottering slightly

on the back step so that Ava had to rush forwards to help her.

'Silly old biddy ...' Nana repeated as she steadied herself and went in. She held on to the wall and Ava watched her until she was safely in the living room.

'Come on,' Robin said, looking at Ava. 'You could do with some cheering up. My treat.'

She led Ava to a cafe round the corner.

'Hiya, Robin, love,' the woman behind the counter said as they went in.

'Hi, Marge,' Robin replied.

Ava allowed Robin to lead her to a table in the window. Marge came over a few minutes later and took their orders.

'A latte for me, please. And a brownie each, cream, the works,' Robin said.

Marge laughed. 'A drink for you, love?' she asked Ava.

'Just a Coke, please.'

'Of course, love. Coming right up.'

The cafe was a cosy space with soft yellow walls covered in cheerful art and shelves lined with books and board games. The brownies Marge brought over were gooey and rich with the warm and buttery scent of vanilla and cream. Robin sipped her latte, a big mug of foamy milk and coffee.

'My little sanctuary,' Robin said of it all. 'I thought we could both do with it.'

Ava smiled.

'Woah! Don't overdo it.'

Then Ava laughed. She took a bite of brownie with cream and felt something warm stir within her. She even closed her eyes and caught herself sighing slightly.

'There we go,' Robin said. 'I knew you couldn't be a moody cow all the time. Sorry. Foot-in-mouth—'

'No,' Ava cut her off. 'This is perfect. Thank you. It's just, you know.'

'What?' Robin asked. She smiled, cheeky, and put on a drawn out, miserable voice for effect. 'Everything seems so pointless?'

Ava shrugged. 'Yeah. It can do.'

Robin arched an eyebrow. 'Not Dustin Marr, though?'

Ava choked on her brownie. Her cheeks coloured. 'What?'

Robin grinned. 'You fancy him, or what? I've seen the way you look at him. The way he looks at you, too.'

Ava folded her arms tightly across her chest. 'It's not like that.'

Robin nodded. She sipped her coffee before carrying on. 'Be careful, Ava. He's a dark one, and mean with it.'

Ava stared down at the table. 'I know.'

She did. She knew it, and she didn't want anything much more to do with Dustin than the rituals because of it. Or she wanted not to want it, if that made sense, which it often didn't, even to herself.

Robin looked at her for a while, then sighed. 'That kind of nihilism is dangerous,' she said.

'That what?'

'Nihilism. The pointlessness. You know, when you don't believe in anything, don't have any kind of compass, don't feel anything good in the world. It can make people feel like they can live by their own rules. Dustin feels that way sometimes, I reckon. The rage and misery eat him up and make him believe that nothing is good, which makes him think there is no such thing as good, which means there's no such thing as bad. You can't have one without the other. And that leads to chaos. It can drive you crazy, make you believe you can do what you want, no matter how violent.'

Robin reached across the table and placed her hand over Ava's.

'It's what makes Dustin Marr so dangerous, I reckon. And I don't want you getting mixed up with it. Or believing it yourself. That pointlessness, that chaos ... sorry. Maybe I'm sticking my nose in where it's not wanted. But I've been worried.'

Ava shook her head. Then she nodded. Robin had put into words what she had been struggling to articulate herself, and she was grateful for it.

'Thank you,' she said. 'You're not sticking your nose in. Or if you are, I'm glad you are. So yeah. Really. Thanks.'

'Always,' Robin promised. She winked. She pulled out a small box from her bag as they finished their cake and slid it across the table to Ava.

'What's this?' Ava asked, surprised.

'It's a little something to keep your spirits up.'

Robin had a mischievous glint in her eyes. Ava opened the box to find a couple of delicate plaited cotton bracelets. Each one had a silver feather woven into it, elegant yet firm.

'I ordered them online,' Robin said.

Ava felt her eyes sting a little.

'They're beautiful,' she whispered. Then she and Robin helped one another put them on. It was a fiddly task, but they got there in the end. Ava looked at her wrist, at the silver feather.

'Sod the crows,' Robin said. 'And sod Dustin Marr. I thought we could be defiant with these. With the feathers. You know? Like they've got no power over us if we're wearing them. What do you think?'

'They're beautiful,' Ava said. 'Beautiful.'

Nineteen

There was going to be a music event at school at the end of term. The head of music, Miss Maple, was calling it Music Fest, and posters had gone up all around school inviting people to put their names down to perform. Each performer would have ten minutes and they could do whatever they wanted. Robin lit up when she saw them.

'Should I put my name down?' she asked.

'Of course you should,' Ava replied. 'You'll be great.'

'You think so?'

'Yeah. Yeah, I do.'

Robin was still nervous, though. 'Can you come with me to sign up?' she asked.

'Of course.'

They went to the music corridor at lunchtime. A few

people were in music lessons. Drums clattered about in one of the practice rooms and someone somewhere hacked and hawed on a violin. The sign-up sheet was outside Miss Maple's classroom door. A few names were already there, a few acts, a couple of soloists.

Robin stood staring at it.

'I don't know . . .'

'I do,' Ava said. She stepped around Robin. There was a ballpoint pen on a string attached to the sign-up sheet and she picked it up and wrote Robin's name in block capitals.

'There, it's done,' she said.

'Oh my God. Oh my God. Do you really think . . . ?'

'Yeah. You'll be great.'

Dustin was being yelled at by a teacher as Ava and Robin went back inside after lunch. She was going on at him about being a vandal and a hooligan, for not respecting anything. Dustin just stood there with his gaze fixed over her shoulder and his face slack.

It must be going round today, Ava thought. Everyone but she and Robin seemed to be wound pretty tight. The air crackled with it. The end of school couldn't come fast enough. She just wanted to run back home and check on Nana. She wanted to see how Pop was doing. She practically sprinted out after the final bell, ready to get home and be away from it all. Robin hurried after her.

'Bridger!' someone shouted.

It was Joe Walder glaring through the sunshine at her.

'There's a ritual on,' he said. 'Dustin's just called it.'

She opened her mouth to speak but Joe Walder was already gone. Half a dozen of the others were tramping up towards the woods in the distance. Ava shook her head, didn't go home to see how everyone was doing, didn't seek the cool and the shade. Instead, she and Robin ran uphill towards the woods and Dustin's ritual.

Twenty

Dustin didn't say anything as they arrived and shuffled over to their places around the hollow. He didn't look at anyone at first, just stared into the drifting smoke. Then he turned to look at Ava when they were all settled in place and she felt a thrill run along her spine.

'You have come for the crows, to hear what they have to say,' Dustin growled, making his way around the circle and touching each person's head as he passed them.

'But the crow's words aren't for everyone . . .'

They all mumbled their replies. Ava looked at the hollow and said 'yes', firm and strong, and she meant it with all her heart, no matter how scared she was. Dustin's hand came to rest on her head, pressing a bit too firmly and sending another chill down her spine.

'The crows bring us close to the dead. You have been chosen,' Dustin whispered solemnly. 'Do you wish to hear what they have to tell you?'

'I do,' she replied.

'Do you swear to listen or else be struck down?'

'I do.'

'Into the flames with you, then.'

And she stood as before and took a step towards the hollow, towards the next life. The fire, the bones, the smoke all took her . . .

The shadows were deeper than before as she stepped out of the hollow in the other world. The air was colder. The crows surrounded her and each seemed to bring dense shadows with them. The shadows thickened and clung all around the clearing, painting it darkly. Ava's breath misted before her.

This is what it is to live in exile. Those voices whispering in her head.

The crow with the white feathers in its wings landed before her. It shimmered. Shadows swelled around it and then Corbie was there. The child with the white streaks in his hair and the voice like an old man stood before her.

This is the cold of forgetting.

'I don't understand,' Ava whispered.

'We don't care,' Corbie croaked, stepping up closer towards her. Ava tried to take a step backwards but found herself rooted to the spot, paralysed, petrified.

'What do you want?'

'AGAIN!' Corbie screeched. It was like a slap across the face. Ava turned from his anger for a second. 'Again . . .' Corbie carried on quietly now, hissing. 'You came to us. It is what you want. Mewling, mewling. You mewl and snivel and beg. Is that it? You're here to beg. It's always what *you* want, isn't it, foolish child?'

'My na—'

'Bah . . .' Corbie hissed. 'We told you. We can give you what you want. We can give the old woman her memories back. But we told you the price.'

'A sacrifice.'

Corbie nodded. He took a step backwards and Ava felt herself freed. She could move her feet once more.

'I should be strong in this world,' Corbie whispered. 'I used to be strong in yours, but I need a footing, a firm hold. Someone who knows all my stories, through whom I can keep my vigil on your world. Stories bridge our worlds, bring the dead to the living and the living to the dead. They have great power. Without someone who knows them, who tells them, breathes new life into them ... I am less, almost nothing. We all are. Shades, barely there.'

'Nana,' Ava said. 'That was Nana, once upon a time.'

Corbie nodded.

'Aye. When she was young and strong. Humans might call her a priestess or something foolish like that. She was our anchor in your world. But now she is old and infirm. Her wits are leaving her—'

'Because you're taking them—'

'SILENCE!'

Ava staggered back a pace. Again, it felt like a physical blow as Corbie shouted.

'We take what we must to ensure that nothing is lost. Your people turned from our world, lived their lives with daughters and granddaughters and damn fool people all around them. Your nana couldn't hold it at bay, couldn't stop people from forgetting. And she took up with that man with his head so full of industry ... cogs and wheels and factories and work... human nonsense.' Pop, Ava thought. They were angry with Pop.

'She had her daughter, her granddaughter,' Corbie spat. 'She had opportunities to elect a successor and yet she didn't pick someone to carry the torch after her. She failed to properly groom someone to take over from her.'

'A successor?'

'The sacrifice.'

It made sense to Ava then.

'That's what you want? You want me to sacrifice myself, to become what . . . your anchor . . . and then you'll give Nana her memories back?'

Crows all around hacked and hawed, cackling. Corbie's good eye blazed.

'No,' he whispered. 'You are not suitable. You cling too much to your own world. You're not open enough to our stories, to the truth of them. It won't do.'

Ava was confused. The crows cackled once more.

'Then what? What . . . who is the sacrifice?'

And then she knew.

'Dustin,' she said.

Corbie nodded.

'We have chosen the boy. He is near perfect. Your nana gave him the gift when he was a boy. She told him all the old stories, the old lore. He was to take her place, but then one day she stopped. She walked away from him.'

'Dustin's dad made it too dangerous to stay,' Ava told him. Corbie shrugged.

'Far more dangerous for her to leave the job part done. He knows much about us and would be a worthy anchor, but he is still too tied to your world. Your nana was too tied to your world, too, and we'll not make that mistake again. The boy could be great, but he is full of rage, and because he is so full of rage he cannot undo those ties. He doesn't yet understand. His soul must be forfeit to the wilds. He must let his anger go and be at peace, otherwise those stories, all that lore, will continue to lose its place in your world. We will take it all back and you will all be made hollow, just like your nana. Soul dead, all of you, in the end.'

'Forfeit?'

'We will take him and he will not be willing at first. He thinks he wants to come. What does he say? He wants *to fly away*. But he deludes himself. He isn't ready or he would have come to us already. It needs to be impossible for him to stay. Only then will he give up on your world and commit fully to ours. We have chosen you, one for whom he cares, who cares for him, to cast him out. He must know that bitterness and then the joy of letting go. So we need you to give him over to us, to sever his place in your world, to send him up into the wilds so that we may get to work.'

She couldn't ever betray someone like that, let alone Dustin. It was an awful thought. And what did they mean, sever?

'You will see what I mean,' Corbie said, appearing as ever to read Ava's thoughts. 'You will betray him when the time comes. You will give him over to us.'

'I won't . . . I couldn't . . .'

'Foolish words, foolish girl. The deal is already made, whether you're willing or not. It's just a matter of time.'

She felt herself dismissed and turned to go, then stopped and turned back to Corbie. He smiled a wicked smile at her.

'Why does it work for me?' she asked. 'The ritual. Why does it work for me, if I'm so tied to life, if I don't know all the old stories? Why me and not Dustin?'

The crows cackled all around her.

'You have known loss, bitter loss,' Corbie whispered.

'My dad?'

Corbie nodded.

'And such loss has shown you a glimpse of our world, the shadow world where we shepherd the dead to the next place. Dustin must come to us, but first he must lose everything.'

Twenty-one

The doctor was there when Ava got home afterwards. She was sitting at the kitchen table with Nana, Pop and Mum, and she smiled sadly at Ava as she came in.

'Love, we won't be long,' Mum said.

Ava rolled her eyes and took her cue, banished. She went up to her bedroom, but the floors were thin enough in these old terraces. She heard the talking, or snatches of it at least. They mentioned dementia, Alzheimer's, cognitive decline. They were words that Ava had heard before. They were all just ways of saying that Nana's memories were leaving her. Just like the crows flying off with her memories was another way of saying it.

Ava closed her eyes as she lay on her bed and she whispered as if speaking to the crows, to Corbie, the young boy with the old voice. She considered what had been asked of her and she sat up late thinking about the crows, about Dustin, about Corbie . . .

Strip it all away, all the nonsense, and all there was in the end was a trade, she realised. Dustin for Nana. Could she do it? Could she bring herself to make that kind of trade, and what would it even mean for Dustin? She didn't know the answers, but she knew what she had to do if she wanted to save Nana, to stop Nana from hollowing out, from losing her soul. If she wanted to bring her back.

It was too much to have been asked, too much to betray someone, to give them over to the crows, whatever that even meant. But then she thought about Nana, about her memory, all those stories lost. And if what Corbie had told her was true then the soul of the whole town or more was at stake.

How could she do it?

But, then again, how could she *not* do it?

'You're horrible, all horrible,' she whispered, thinking of the crows. She heard wingbeats outside and far-off caws that sounded all too much like laughter.

Twenty-two

Mum took Ava out for breakfast a couple of days later. They walked around to Marge's cafe, just the two of them.

'It's nice in there, you'll see,' Ava told Mum.

'Yeah? There was never anything that good around here when I was growing up. Crawford must be coming up in the world.'

Marge was happy to see them. 'Find a table, my dears,' she called out from behind the counter. 'I'll come and get your orders in a bit.'

The place was heaving. The smell of bacon and fried eggs lay heavy over everything. They settled at a table at the back and looked at the menu. Mum decided on eggs and bacon with something called hollandaise sauce and a toasted muffin. 'Eggs benedict,' she called it. Ava went for a bacon roll with extra ketchup.

'You're Miriam and Tom's daughter, right?' Marge asked Mum as she scribbled their orders on a little notepad.

'Yes. I'm Evelyn. And this is Ava.'

'Oh, I know Ava.' Marge winked at Ava, gave her a big smile. Then she looked at Mum. 'I was very sorry to hear about Miriam. You know, her memory. She was such a sharp cookie. Too sharp sometimes.'

'Don't I know it,' Mum replied. She smiled sadly up at Marge. 'Thank you,' she said.

Marge left to get their order ready, and Ava watched Mum as she traced the rim of her mug with a finger. She's stressed, she realised.

'You OK, Mum?'

'Huh?' Mum looked a little startled. She had been in her own world. 'Yeah, I'm fine. Fine enough, I guess.'

'But not really fine,' Ava said.

Mum chuckled.

'Pretty much. It's just all been such a lot, hasn't it? And, honestly, I wasn't ready for your nana. For her being so far gone. I had no idea it was so bad and it's all sort of hit all at once. Your dad, the move, new school and job each . . . and Nana. It's a lot.'

Ava felt her eyes grow a little warm. Her throat tightened. She thought about Dustin and the crows and the betrayal she suspected could fix so much of it, and she just nodded.

'Yeah,' she said quietly. 'Yeah.'

Ava went to school feeling mixed up about it all. Anger and frustration still lay heavily over the whole of St Francis', in fact. Or at least so it seemed to her. Even Miss Faulkner glowered as she took the morning register. Sunshine poured in through every window, bleaching the world white, and everybody snapped at everybody else.

Luke Jenkins was out in the sunshine showing off at lunchtime, playing a few tunes as some of his admirers sat around listening. Ava scowled at him from across the yard. Dustin walked past, grimacing.

'Look at the caveman go!' Luke called out. He felt safe surrounded by all these people in the sunshine. The idiot, Ava thought. They all laughed at Dustin, and Dustin froze and then turned and barged through the crowd. He squared his shoulders and pushed his way forwards as people fled. Luke was confident. Ava had no idea why. Perhaps he felt safe surrounded by people, with teachers close at hand. Or maybe he was just angry like everyone else that day, and foolhardy with it. He spat in Dustin's face and went to shove him, but Dustin was having none of it. He grunted and reached out with one hand, snatched Luke's guitar away, and smashed Luke around the head with it. No matter how skinny Dustin was, he was strong, strong in a feral, animal way that sent Luke flying.

Luke staggered backwards and landed sprawled in the grass.

Ava swore. She was already moving forwards. Dustin dropped the broken guitar and went in towards Luke, getting ready to kick him where he lay, but Ava stepped up to him. She stood between him and Luke and squared her own shoulders, small though she was, and Dustin stopped.

'What are you doing?' he snapped.

'Stopping you from doing something really stupid,' she replied.

People were coming to watch. Luke lay half-forgotten on the ground. Miss Faulkner and a few other teachers were a little way off, frowning over at them as they realised that something was going on. Dustin didn't see any of it, though. He was far too angry. He seemed to Ava to swell with it, and she noticed too late the red mark at his throat, the purpling around his eye.

'Your dad been knocking you about?' she asked softly. 'It's OK—'

Dustin made an animal noise in the back of his throat. Muscles bunched in his jaw and his eyes flashed with a cold fury. He bared his teeth and reached forwards to where Luke was getting to his feet, tried to push past Ava to get at him.

'No,' she said. She stayed in front of him and gritted her teeth. 'Don't do it.'

'Don't tell me what to do!' Dustin growled.

He barged past her, knocking her back a few feet. She stumbled and found herself on one knee, unbalanced. Then it was too late. Luke was back on his feet and squaring up nervously to Dustin. He swore at Dustin, came in to shove him back, but he simply bounced backwards as he pushed. Dustin laughed harshly and jumped, leaped, tackling Luke to the ground.

'Stop it!' Ava shouted. 'Stop!'

She was dimly aware of Robin running over and

shouting. Far off voices rose in alarm. Charging feet smacked the ground, but they were quickly drowned out. It was all drowned out.

All Ava could hear was the beating of wings, thunderous wings, wings overhead and everywhere, all around.

You need our help.

I do. But I can't.

You can. Give him to us and we will save you from him.

I can't.

There was murder in Dustin's eyes. He looked like he was capable of tearing the whole world apart around him. Robin tried to pull Dustin off Luke, said something that Ava didn't catch. Dustin didn't hear it, didn't seem to know what was going on around him as he held Luke down. Then Robin was down, tripping as Dustin and Luke tousled, and they were on top of her as they fought.

She was in danger. Robin was in danger.

Say it.

It was agony. She didn't want to play their game, didn't want to betray Dustin, didn't want to betray anyone. But Dustin had lost all control and was about to hurt someone and she didn't think anything else could stop him.

Say it.

Robin. Robin was helpless. Dustin and Luke's fight was about to hurt her. Ava's feelings for him aside, he was a beast. He was dangerous. The betrayal, the sacrifice ... the fate of the town rested on it, the fate of all their souls, and now he deserved it. He deserved it.

Damn him, she thought. I damn him, I condemn him.

Say it.

'Help me,' Ava whispered.

You will let us have him?

'I will.'

You do?

'I do.'

The crows laughed.

Accepted. We will take him.

Those wings beat harder. Ava stood with an effort and looked around. The crows circled her, a writhing tornado of black feathers, sharp beaks, grasping talons, and awful, brilliant, white-hot eyes. They stood between her and Dustin, who jumped to his feet as he saw them come. His own anger was fast beginning to falter. Fear remained and little else. He was stammering as the crows descended. Robin rolled and scuttled back from it all with her own eyes wide in terror, and Luke simply lay there in the grass watching.

A couple of crows dive bombed Dustin, splattering him with their white mess. Then another swooped in, bolder than the rest, with its talons outstretched. It dug those talons into Dustin's scalp and drops of blood fell behind it as it swept away. It came to land by Ava, cawing loudly.

Dustin shouted out. He turned and tried to run but the crows were everywhere. They churned around him and Ava. Feathers flew and beaks clacked. They dove and they cut, they messed and they cawed. Talons and whiteness and red, red blood swirled about, and Ava felt her own anger sing with it all. It welled up in her and extended beyond her and the crows flew through it, lifted by it and swept along like it was the very wind beneath their wings. They dealt in stories and hers was one of pain and rage and she saw it reflected in them as they attacked.

Dustin staggered down onto one knee. His shirt was ripped. His hair was slick, red and white, blood and mess. He cried out a primal scream and the sound cut through the whirl of birds and the beating of their wings against the air. It cut through to Ava, startled her, snapped her out of it.

What have I done?

'Enough,' she said.

The hurricane ended. The crows grew calm very suddenly.

Most of them landed between Ava and Dustin. They cawed a little and then fell silent. Everything was silent except for the sound of Dustin breathing hard like a wounded animal. His whole body was wet with blood and mess, with his own sweat, rich with fear.

Twenty-three

What have I done?

Ava asked herself the same question over and over in the days that followed.

What have I done?

He would have stayed for Ava, even if he was expelled for attacking Luke. She knew it. Her betrayal had left him with nothing. Less than nothing, bitter and cast out, so he would leave for the wilds with a will. Willing, eager to run. The crows could now do what they needed with him and to him.

Robin was bruised and dazed, though she was otherwise fine. The same was true of Ava, too, though her shoulder ached a little. She was mostly just shaken. The crows had their claim over Dustin. They would have his soul. She knew it with a certainty. She knew that she had allowed it to happen . . . caused it to happen . . . betrayed him.

What have I done?

Pop and Jeanie were there by the time they were done speaking to the head teacher, waiting outside her office to take them home. Mrs Doherty took statements from them both as the school nurse looked them over, told them everything would be OK.

Mum arrived home from work an hour or so after they got back. 'Oh, love,' she said when she saw Ava.

The phone rang a little while later and Ava heard Mum shouting, firm in a way she hadn't heard her be for a long time. Not since Dad's death, at least. Then the phone went again ten minutes later and Ava heard Mum greeting Mrs Doherty. They had a long conversation as Ava sat in her room, just able to hear Mum's voice on the phone. Mum came up afterwards to speak to her.

'Am I in trouble?' Ava asked.

'Not at all, my love.' Mum sat next to Ava on her bed. 'You were the victims, you and Robin, and the other boy, this Luke,' she said quietly. 'None of you did anything wrong. That . . . beast, Dustin Marr, started it all. Everyone knows what he's like, and they know he would've done more if . . . if he could have.'

Mum sounded a little disturbed by it all.

'What's going to happen?' Ava asked.

'Well, we'll keep you off school tomorrow,' Mum said. 'I've spoken to Jeanie and she's doing the same with Robin.'

'And Dustin?'

Mum smiled ruefully.

'I heard from his dad,' she said. 'That was him on the phone before Mrs Doherty.'

Ava nodded. The shouting made sense now.

'He was trying to threaten me with all sorts, the drunken fool,' Mum carried on. 'He reckons you set the crows on Dustin.'

Ava looked away guiltily, but Mum didn't seem to notice anything.

'I told him that it was preposterous, of course,' Mum said. 'I threatened to call the police if he tried to get in touch with me again. Mrs Doherty was more helpful about it all, of course. She told me that Luke and Dustin have been to hospital. Luke's fine, just a little bruised. Dustin's OK, too. They cleaned him up, disinfected his cuts, gave him a couple of stitches. Nothing too bad.'

'What's going to happen to him?' Ava asked. She needed him to be OK, otherwise it would be true. She would have sold him to the wild places, made him an outcast.

'He's been suspended,' Mum said. 'I don't know what will happen to him in the long run, though Mrs Doherty told me that she thinks there's no place for someone like him at St Francis'.'

Ava's heart sank. It was all going as the crows had said it would. Dustin was having his ties to this world cut. An outcast, chucked out of school and hated by all. There was nothing much to stop him from running for the wilds and Ava knew deep down that that's exactly what was going to happen. He was going to go.

They sat in stillness for a moment, then Mum took a deep breath. She took Ava's hand in her own.

'Love . . .' she began.

'Yeah?'

'What exactly happened? People are talking about the birds, the crows . . . they're saying they seemed to . . . intervene in the fight, that they stood between you and Dustin at the end.'

Ava nodded.

'Yeah,' she said. 'It's like in Nana's stories. They're watching over us or something. Over me . . .' She couldn't say much more. She couldn't tell her that she had sold Dustin out.

'I don't know,' she said with a sigh.

Twenty-four

'How are you doing?'

Robin shrugged. 'It's not great. But it'll be OK, especially now Dustin's gone.'

Ava wasn't so sure. She couldn't be happy about Dustin, about what she had done to him. Robin didn't notice her discomfort. She just held Ava firmly in her gaze.

'The crows,' she said.

'Yeah?'

'What happened? What the hell?'

Ava shrugged. 'I don't know. All I know is that they had my back, they wanted to stop Dustin from hurting me, hurting us . . .'

She took a deep breath and shook her head.

'No,' she said. 'That's not it. Not all of it.'

She had to tell someone. It was too much of a burden to carry. It pressed against her like an invisible weight, making the air around feel thick as she swallowed pain and worry. She had to speak.

'They offered me a deal...'

She told Robin everything, everything that had happened during the rituals. 'I made the deal when I saw him and Luke fighting with you in the middle of it all. They came, they protected us and took him. And then I wanted them to be done and they stopped.'

They were both quiet for a long time. Then, after a while, Robin looked at Ava with a curious expression and clearly decided on something. 'You still, you know... like him?' she asked. 'Even after yesterday?'

Ava felt herself blush. Then she let out a deep sigh and nodded slightly. It felt good unburdening herself, so she figured she might as well go all the way.

'Yeah, I do.' She bit her lip. 'I really do,' she said. 'But.'

'But what?'

Ava felt uncomfortable. She hated talking about feelings, and, she admitted to herself, she hated how she felt about Dustin. She didn't want to fancy him. He was older, and he was mean and aggressive, and dark... and, worst of all, she had near enough sent him reeling into a different world.

'But it's more complicated than that. There's so much more going on between us than just that.'

'What do you mean? The ritual? Or the fact that he tried to beat Luke to a pulp at school, with me thrown into the bargain?'

Ava's belly flared with anger, defensive, but she calmed down as she looked up at Robin. It was a good point.

'Kind of, yeah,' she conceded. 'Yeah. All of that. And also . . . well, we've got a bond.'

She and Dustin felt tied to one another. By the crows, because of the choice they had given Ava, of course. But also, it was like there had been a bond from the first time they had met. That's why the crows had felt able to force the choice on Ava. Their bond meant that she really could sacrifice him and have it mean something.

She shook her head. She didn't know.

'I don't know how to describe it,' she told Robin.

'I've seen it,' Robin replied. 'I know what you mean.'

'Yeah?'

Robin simply nodded.

'Yeah,' Ava said. 'So fancying him, or whatever . . . it's

the least important thing right now. It doesn't matter, not compared to the rest of it.'

'You're not bothered about him being, you know, violent? Because you should be. His behaviour isn't OK.'

Ava nodded. 'I know. I don't like the violence. Actually, I hate it, and I wouldn't ever want to, you know, go out with him because of it . . . I fancy him for what he could be, I think. Maybe for what he will be, not for what he is right now. And I'd never do anything about it till I was sure he had learned to . . . you know . . .'

'Behave himself?' Robin offered, arching an eyebrow.

'Control himself. Control the darkness in him. Or make peace with it. I'm not sure. Does that make sense?'

Robin took a deep breath. 'OK,' she said. 'But I also know you a bit, I think, and I think you'll always bring this . . . I don't know. Heaviness? You'll always make it complicated. And I get it. It is complicated. But, well, maybe sometimes things don't need to be so complicated. Sometimes the boy you like is just the boy you like.'

Ava chuckled and looked at Robin. 'Surely you don't approve? You of all people. You hate Dustin.'

'Hate's a strong word, but yeah, I don't like him. I think he's mean. He *is* mean, and I'm not interested in forgiving him. But if you like him . . .' Robin shrugged. '*Carpe diem,*' she said.

'What?'

'It's Latin. Dad told me. It means *seize the day*. Which means, basically, that life is short, so do what you need to do. I think.'

Ava thought about it. It's not something she had ever really thought about, though Dad used to say that life was short. The irony hit Ava then. Or maybe not irony, but something. Life was short. His life had been short in the end. Seize the day . . . make the most of it all. She knew she certainly didn't. It was hard to do when you felt like she did. It was hard to do when you were so depressed and angry. But she looked at Robin and thought, OK, yeah. Seize the day. Maybe she would be able to one day.

Twenty-five

Nobody had seen any sign of Dustin since the fight. None of the others had heard anything from him. They stood around talking about him at break and lunch, swapping rumours. Everyone seemed to agree that he had left town, gone up into the woods, begun to live in the wild, though no one knew quite where the rumours had begun.

They've taken him, Ava thought. The crows have him now.

Ava felt foolish, used. The guilt got to her, guilt over selling Dustin out, no matter how much he might have deserved it in the moment. The worst part was that it seemed to be for nothing. Dustin was gone, in the crows' world, in their grasp. She had upheld her part in the bargain, despite how horrible it made her feel, but Nana was worse, if anything, and getting worse all the time.

One day, Nana came into the living room and sat down when it was just Ava in there. Coldness followed her in, coldness and shadow.

'Where's your dad?' she asked. 'I've not seen him in days. It's not like him.'

Ava's throat caught. Her eyes stung. Nana just sat there looking at her with a slightly bemused look on her face.

'Nana . . . Dad . . . he died,' Ava mumbled. 'A couple of years ago.'

'Oh no,' Nana said. She pouted and frowned. 'Oh, that's a pity. He was such a sweet thing. The loveliest son-in-law we could ever have asked for.' Then she brightened. 'Still, never mind,' she said breezily. 'I'm sure he'll be back soon enough, then we'll be able to put this nonsense behind us.'

'Maybe, Nana,' Ava said quietly. 'Maybe.'

She cursed the crows.

'You were meant to fix her, give her back her memories,' she whispered to the night. 'You were meant to make things better.'

They hadn't. Nothing had changed.

Twenty-six

The air crackled as Ava watched. It vibrated. Robin's eyes were wide and half-wild as she stood there.

She raised her voice to a higher pitch and swam through the next verse. It was lovely, beautiful, Ava thought. They were in an old set of ruins. It was one of Jay's favourite spots, Robin said, up in the woods and far from anywhere, deserted enough that Robin could practise for Music Fest as loud as she wanted without anyone hearing.

'Come up there with me,' she had told Ava. 'I want to try it all out on you, so you can tell me if I should go ahead with it or not.'

She ended her song. It was all her own work, and Ava liked it a lot. She thought it was wild and jagged, really punchy, and it made her feel alive, infatuated with life.

There was a lot of rage in there, she thought, mingling with the beauty. Then it seemed to Ava to all flow flawlessly into sweetness with the next song. Robin stood completely still and her voice grew deep and slow and mournful.

'My sweet brother, it's time you found your bed.
Your world is full of wonder, but in the end,
It's over, finished. It's time to rest your head.
Go sweetly now and dream, my friend.'

Ava was completely mesmerised by it. Electrified.

There were tears in Robin's eyes as she finished. She wiped them on the back of her sleeve and glowered at Ava.

'It's rubbish, isn't it?' she snapped. 'Go on, say it. You hated it.'

Ava shook her head. 'It's beautiful,' she said. 'I loved it.'

'Yeah, well, it's not fully finished yet. It needs more work.'

'No, it . . .'

'But I've got a few weeks left. I'll get it right. This is just a rough draft.' She paused and sniffed. 'It's about Jay,' she said.

'I know,' Ava replied. She had guessed as much from the lyrics, but also from Robin's obvious emotion as she had sung. It made Ava's own heart ache for Dad.

'It wasn't too bad?'

'Honestly, it was great,' Ava told her, and she meant it.

'Well . . . OK. But remember, it's just a draft.'

'I know. But still.'

Robin's songs stuck with Ava all afternoon and all evening. They carried on rolling through her head when she went to bed that night, mixing in with memories of Dad. They were in her dreams until her dreams were interrupted. Hurried footsteps crashed around on the landing. Ava took a moment, caught between dreaming and sleep, and then her heart skipped a beat. The footsteps were accompanied by the faint sound of shouting.

Ava was wide awake immediately as Mum opened her door.

'Love, your nana's gone,' Mum said.

'What?'

'She's gone.'

They all got dressed quickly and hurried out into the street. The sun was peeping over the rooftops, up early as summer rolled on. A few people were about, though not many. It was mostly just quiet and empty streets.

'Go round the block,' Mum said. 'She can't have gone far.'

They split up. Pop headed off round the corner, his eyes wide in panic. Mum rushed up the street, looking left and right. Ava looked all about. The street felt too big, too empty, as if it might swallow her whole. A car crawled past with headlights glaring in the dusk, its engine too loud, too sharp. A dog barked somewhere distant and the sound cut through the cold air. A young woman in a dark hoodie walked briskly on the other side of the road with her head down and her hands buried in her pockets. Every shadow stretched too long and every movement felt too sudden.

A crow settled on a wall a little way along the street. *Come, come,* it seemed to beckon her. Then it took off and flew a circle and headed away. Ava followed. Her skin prickled, her hands were clammy, as if the whole world had tilted and she was the only one who didn't know how to keep her balance. She ran along out of the streets, up the meadow on the way towards the blackforest and the hills beyond. Her feet squelched through the dewy grass until they were soaked through. Her legs and lungs burned as she sprinted up to the treeline and she thought, *No, no, no, don't let anything happen to Nana, my nana. Please, please.* Her heart felt like it might burst with anxiety.

Hurry, hurry, the crow seemed to say. It was agitated. *It's not yet time for the end.* More crows gathered. They whirled around and glared at her. She felt like she could hardly breathe, she was so scared. Then something snapped and her fear turned to rage.

'Where is she?' Ava shouted up at them.

The whirlwind of feathers buckled. It broke as she shouted.

'You promised she'd be OK, you promised!'

She shouted and screamed. The crows' eyes flashed. The feathers in their wings rustled. She shouted again and again as a dark heat rose in her limbs and face. It felt good. She felt powerful as she shouted.

'Arghhh!' she screamed at the birds. She raged and they began to peel away. The outer ones fled, disappearing into the blackforest's shadows. Ava tingled and her head grew light and her vision swam a little, but she kept at it.

Shouting and screaming.

Screaming and shouting.

More birds peeled away. They disappeared into the

shadows, retreating, shocked by the strength of her emotion. Everything came out of her as she bellowed her fury at them. She raged at her dad for dying. Raged and raged, so angry with him that it brought tears to her eyes, stinging as they ran down her cheeks. She raged at the world for carrying on without him. *Don't you know he died? Don't you know that the most important man in the world just died one day and you didn't even blink?* No one did. The whole planet just kept on turning and turning with all its stupid, horrible little people on it. The Earth's crust should have shattered the day he died. The heavens should have opened and thunder and lightning should have poured from them, lashing at the ground now that he was gone. Everyone everywhere should have fallen to their knees sobbing because Dad was gone and the world was broken.

And now Nana's losing her memories ... no, having them stolen... and you promised. You promised.

She screamed and she shouted but nobody cared.

'Don't you know that MY DAD DIED?'

She wanted to punch and kick and scratch. She wanted to hurt the world like she had been hurt just so she knew that it knew her pain.

'Don't you know that MY NANA IS DISAPPEARING?'

The air shimmered around her as Ava fell to her knees and the birds darted away from all her anger and hurt. And then Nana was there. Ava realised after a little while that she had come down to her from the blackforest. She had her arms around Ava and was pulling her back towards the town, making silly shushing noises like she could make it all OK, like she could take the anger away.

Nothing can take the anger away, though. Nothing.

Because my dad died and the world kept on going.

She was only half aware of what was happening. She found herself back at the house soon enough, sitting at the kitchen table and sobbing like she had never thought she could sob. Her throat hurt and her chest hurt and every muscle in her body spasmed and heaved.

Nana was there. So was Pop. So was Mum. Of course Mum was there.

Mum was always there.

'Oh my love,' Mum said, and she held Ava tight.

'Corbie got me for a moment, then,' Nana whispered as Ava's sobbing died down at last. 'But then I heard this one. The young calling out, the living not done with me just yet.'

Twenty-seven

Ava was shattered after her early morning excursion to find Nana, after screaming at the birds, after releasing all that emotion. They sat around in the kitchen for a bit and then Mum told her to go back to bed.

'Just for a couple of hours, love. You'll feel better for it.'

She was asleep quickly enough and immediately fell into a strange and vivid dream. Corbie came to her after all that rage. It felt like he had decided on something. Decided to honour their deal at last, perhaps.

First, he was carved of wood and flying awkwardly. He kept having to land as his wings failed him. She chased him and caught up.

'Hey, hey!' she shouted.

He turned and fixed her with his good eye and she

took a deep breath. Then he was made of smoke and he billowed effortlessly through the air. The smoke was from Dustin's ritual, wafting up through pine branches to fill the clearing, to cover the sky over Crawford. She herself flew down from the smoke, back into the clearing, and saw her name and Dustin's etched into the cairn. The other names were all gone. It felt like they had never really been there at all. The smoke-Corbie then came down and drifted along into the woods and Ava followed. Corbie showed her to the hills above and a ridge of granite furrowed from the land. She expected to find her dad sheltering there. She certainly felt him, but it was fleeting. There was nobody there. All she saw was a spent fire, ash and dust, with Dustin's staff lying next to it.

It was where he had been living.

It's all coming together, Corbie croaked in his old man's voice. *Now's the time to go to him, see for yourself what you have wrought.*

She stood with Corbie in her dream even as she began to feel herself waking up.

'Why Nana and Dustin?' she asked. She realised that it had been bothering her. Nothing much connected them, except that Nana had once babysat him. Corbie laughed.

She chose him when he was young.

'But why? They're so different!'

Less different than you imagine. Both are enthralled by stories, by the old lore. Both like to drink deep of that well. We all live in stories, all of my kind and all of yours, but few like those two. Few indeed. And it's what we need.

And Ava was awake as Corbie's high cackling rang in her ears and then faded.

Nana was in the kitchen when she went down around ten. 'There are strange rumours going around about last night,' she told Ava. Her eyes were clear and sharp for the moment.

'What?' Ava asked. 'What about last night?'

'About the Marrs. There was a fight at the Marr place, people are saying. I just had it from Jeanie.'

Danny Marr had been seen being led off in handcuffs. Dustin Marr had been seen, too, some said. Others said he was gone. Some said he was dead, killed by his own father. All anyone knew for sure was that Eileen Marr, Dustin's mother, was on her own in the cottage and that Danny Marr was locked up and that Dustin could be anywhere or nowhere.

'Strange rumours, strange boy ... a strange family, that one ...'

Nana's eyes dimmed. She faded and then simply sat and smiled pleasantly at Ava.

Ava knew where he was. That was what her dream had been about. She packed a bag and went up into the woods late in the afternoon. It began to rain lightly as she walked along. Clouds gathered black in the sky and cast the whole world into twilight. She had a backpack full to the brim with tins and cans and packets of crisps, enough to keep someone going for a week or so. She had no doubt that she would be able to find Dustin. The crows would see to it. She knew it with a certainty that wasn't so strange to her these days.

They began to fly along overhead as she approached the treeline at the usual spot. Ava followed them as they soared low, their black wings cutting through the afternoon's dank light as jagged shadows against that harsh grey sky. They moved as one, a silent procession.

She headed to the ritual site first. Her dream had taken her there so somehow it seemed right. There was no one and nothing there other than the hole in the ground, now empty, and the cairn, standing there with all their names on it. Ava went poking around a bit and found something in the leaves. She bent down and picked it up.

Dustin's necklace. The skull, the feathers.

The crows circled and flitted, half seen in the trees' shadows and their reaching boughs. Ava put the necklace in her pocket and left the clearing and followed, as in her dream, up into the woods.

The trees closed more tightly. They crowded in around her. A few crows swooped down, however. They sped through the trees and it seemed to Ava as though the trees parted for them, shifting across a little bit, bending away slightly so that a slim pathway opened up.

Come, come, the crows seemed to say. Then they were gone, leaving Ava to hurry along after them.

They came to the hills soon enough. The narrow track the crows had been taking her along through the trees started to zigzag upwards and Ava's legs began to burn. Her breathing became laboured. And then, suddenly, the trees vanished from around her and she broke out into the open air. She found herself in a wide-open clearing, facing a wall of cliffs in the middle distance as the rain pattered about. A dark silhouette stood a little way off, glaring at her.

Dustin.

Twenty-eight

Dustin wasn't as pale as he had been. Living rough had given his skin a little colour, a little vibrance, though his eyes had deep rings under them. He looked half wild to Ava, like he had taken a step away from humanity and begun to become something more . . . feral. She supposed it was exactly what the crows had wanted, after all. The hair sweeping back from his face was longer, almost down to his shoulders.

It suited him, she thought.

A few crows wheeled and cawed and came back to them. They landed a little way off and watched Ava and Dustin. Dustin glared at Ava and she glared at him and there they stood, ten feet apart as a dozen crows eyed them through the rain.

'Really, how do you do it?' Dustin asked, looking at them.

Ava just laughed. It wasn't a kind sound. The last time she had seen Dustin he had hurt her and he had hurt Robin, so she had no desire to be kind, no matter how guilty she felt.

Dustin grunted and led her over to the cliffs. The crows watched, still and silent. The cliffs had an overhanging bit of rock at one point. It looked like a great, frowning brow to Ava. The cliff face beneath it was slightly hollowed out, making a kind of shelter. The cave from her dream. It was littered with bits. A sleeping bag, an old dead fire, some clothes, some empty tins. A few bits of carved wood.

'This is where you've been living,' Ava said.

Dustin didn't reply. He just sat down on the rumpled sleeping bag and took a knife out of his pocket. He picked up a piece of wood and began whittling and carving, running the blade along it so that ribbons peeled off. He gathered the ribbons together and placed them on the old fire, then set a tepee of sticks around the little bundle. He took out a lighter and clicked it on and set the flame against the ribbons. The whole lot began to smoulder, and

Dustin blew on it until a small flame crackled into life. He built it up so that soon enough the cave was warm and bright. Ava began to steam slightly as she sat down opposite Dustin with the fire between them, and her wet clothes began to dry.

Dustin sat in stillness, staring at the flames and idly carving away at the wood, shaping it. He looked almost peaceful, far more peaceful than she had ever seen him look before.

'You ever feel that heaviness in you?' he asked in a low voice without preamble after a while. 'That emptiness that still manages to sit like a rock in your stomach.'

Ava didn't say anything, but she knew the feeling very well. It had haunted her these past couple of years ever since her dad's death.

Dustin nodded. He understood.

'It had begun to get worse for me.' Dustin looked up from the flames and stared at Ava levelly. 'There's nothing to life, is there? No meaning, really. No point. Nothing matters, and it makes all of us look like a joke.'

'Everything turns to nothing in the end,' Ava whispered, agreeing with him as she thought about her dad.

Dustin nodded. He spat into the fire and swore. The spit sizzled and baked off. He glared at Ava and something in his face gave. Something in his jaw loosened a little.

'Do you really believe it?' he asked. 'That there's no point?'

Ava thought about the depression she had felt after Dad's death. She thought about Robin. *Carpe diem.* She shrugged. 'I don't know,' she said. 'Sometimes, yeah. Not all the time, though. I don't know.'

Dustin nodded. He slid his knife extra hard and a piece of the wood he was carving split off. Ava watched his hands as they worked.

'I heard about your dad getting arrested,' she said after a bit. She didn't say any more, just let it hang there.

'Yeah,' he said. He looked at her like he guessed what she was thinking. 'I'm glad. Nothing else, really. He belongs behind bars.'

She nodded. Fair enough.

'What happened?' she asked. 'You were there, weren't you?'

'Yeah, I was.'

'So?'

'So we fought,' Dustin said. 'What more do you want?'

He looked at her and glared. Then he sighed.

'Fine,' he said. 'I went back to pick up some new bones. You know, the crows, the barn. But Dad saw me. He went ballistic and tried to take a swing at me. But I took a swing back, knocked him on his arse.' He smiled, clearly relishing the memory. 'We fought and I left. I guess Mum must have called the police because I could hear the sirens as I headed off back towards the woods.'

He sat quietly for a while.

'You sent me up here,' he said after a long while.

'Sort of.'

'What do you mean, sort of?'

'The crows asked me to offer you up to them, so you could ... I don't know, help make them a part of this world. But I didn't want to do it. I don't think I was going to, though I'm not sure.'

'What changed?'

'You attacked Luke. You put Robin in danger, even if you didn't mean to. They gave me a chance to keep her safe from you, to stop the fighting, but it meant inviting them in. It meant letting them take you.'

'And who are you that you can offer me up like that? Don't I get a say in it?'

'No,' she said. 'Or you didn't then. I think you do now. What you do next is up to you, isn't it?'

'Is it?' Dustin shook his head. He glanced out into the night, out to where the crows were standing, watching. 'They're already part of this world,' he said.

'The crows are, sure. But it's about Corbie.'

'Oh.'

He nodded. He understood.

'He needs a foot in this world,' Ava told him. 'Or a representative. You know, a priest or something, I guess.'

'And that's me?'

'Yeah. It was my nana. They've chosen you to take over. I think she chose you. That's why she told you all those old stories. But, you know . . .'

'Yeah. Dad made it so she couldn't look after me any more and she abandoned me.'

'I think she needed to.'

'Hm.'

'You don't find this all weird?'

'I would've, once,' Dustin said.

'Not now?'

'Not so much, no.' He paused and then growled the next few words. 'Don't tell my mum where I am. Don't tell anyone. I'll know if you do and I'll be gone long before anyone gets here. I need to be alone. Do you understand? Alone.'

Ava nodded. She understood.

He grunted and then reached into his pocket and pulled out a small, white oval of wood which he passed to her. It looked like some kind of bone. No, she thought. An egg, a bird's egg. He had whittled it smooth and carved a crow's face into it.

'Just give her this. My mum,' he said. 'It should stop her worrying too badly.'

Then he stood and jutted his chin to the outside world, back at the woods. Ava felt herself dismissed, so she stood too. She turned to go and then stopped. She opened her rucksack and tipped the contents out on the ground. Tins of food and cans of drink and everything else came to rest by the fire.

'You can't survive on nicking things or whatever you've been doing,' Ava told him. 'This will keep you going for a bit.'

Dustin sneered and spat. He stared out past the fire, behind her and beyond her. 'I'm glad you got me kicked out of school,' he said. 'I'm free now. I've got that to share with the crows at least. Maybe now I can become like them. Maybe I can be like Corbie, or whatever. I'm free like they are. I can just fly away. Maybe remember. Maybe hear their stories, speak to them. Or maybe not. I don't know, don't care. I'm free, is all.'

Ava didn't know what to say. Dustin certainly looked freer, or calmer at least. The anger, the hatred, all was dimmed. She just shook her head and zipped up her bag and threw it over her shoulder. She turned to go, then took a deep breath and looked at Dustin for a second.

'You got yourself kicked out of school,' she told him.

'And you sold me out.'

She took a deep breath. 'Yeah.'

'Just so we know where we stand,' he said. His voice was so quiet she could barely hear it. 'Neither of us gets off the hook.'

Ava held onto his necklace, didn't tell him that she had found it. Then she was gone, back towards the trees as the rain continued to patter around her.

'Something's changed in the house,' Nana said that evening. She looked at Ava and arched her eyebrow like it had something to do with her. Ava simply nodded and headed upstairs. She rooted around in her backpack and came down a minute later with the necklace.

'Oh my,' Nana said as Ava handed it to her. She fingered it and sighed. 'Strong stuff.'

Then she looked up and stared hard into Ava's eyes.

'You have suffered,' she said. It wasn't a question. She knew it, even if she couldn't always remember why.

'Yes, Nana,' Ava replied. 'I have. We all have.'

'Oh, my dear, my love.'

Nana fingered the necklace a little more, held the skull in the palm of her hand, and brushed her fingertips against the smaller bones and the remaining feathers.

'You are strong,' Nana told Ava. 'It is going to be a good year, now. When all is said and done. A good year.'

'I hope so, Nana.'

'Oh, Evelyn,' Nana sighed. 'Always so strong.'

Twenty-nine

'Not long now till the solstice,' Nana said the next morning. 'The longest day of the year.'

'She always observes it,' Pop said. 'Have I ever told you what an old pagan she is?'

He chuckled and sipped his tea.

Ava went to find Eileen Marr that morning. She forged a doctor's note and headed over to Dustin's cottage instead of going to her first few lessons. In the end, though, she bumped into Eileen Marr about a quarter of a mile from the cottage. It was obvious who she was. She looked a lot like her son, all high cheekbones, moody scowling, marble beauty. Ava thought that she was only half looking where she was going and not seeing much. The sunlight beat down all around her but she didn't seem to feel a thing. Ava walked up to her and put a hand on her arm and it was only then that she snapped out of it. She leaped backwards and glared at Ava. Then she narrowed her eyes some more.

'I know you,' she said. 'You were one of the ones who got Dustin kicked out of school.'

Ava shook her head. 'No,' she said. 'He got himself kicked out. But yeah, I was there when he and Luke Jenkins fought. Before, you know . . .'

'The crows.'

'Yeah.'

Something seemed to dawn on Eileen Marr, then.

'That means you're Miriam's granddaughter,' she said.

'I am.'

'Oh, love,' Eileen Marr said. She visibly softened. 'Oh, I was so sorry to hear about your nana. About what she's going through. You'll never know how much she meant to me and Dustin when he was a boy.'

'I know,' Ava replied. 'She taught you both all her stories. And I think they'll keep Dustin safe in the end.'

'Maybe,' Eileen said.

'Definitely.'

Ava hesitated and then took a breath. 'I've seen him,' she said.

Eileen Marr squinted at her. Then her eyes went wide.

'Oh, my. Oh, love. Where?'

'Yesterday,' Ava said. 'Up in the woods, but I can't say exactly where for sure. He asked me to give you this.' She handed Eileen Marr the carved egg. Eileen Marr's eyes misted over as she took it and held it up. She smiled and her shoulders relaxed.

'Corbie,' she whispered. Then she looked at Ava. 'He's with the birds and beyond me for now. But he's safe.'

'He is,' Ava replied.

'Thank you, thank you,' Eileen Marr whispered. Ava felt a wrench in her stomach, guilt as ever for her betrayal.

'It's . . . it's nothing,' she said. 'Really.'

'It's everything,' Eileen Marr replied.

There was an ambulance at home when Ava got back after school that afternoon. A couple of paramedics were steering Nana into the back of it on a bed on wheels. She had a mask over her face and Pop was hovering over her looking terrified.

The stairs up to the bathroom had been getting too

hard for Nana to manage and she had messed herself a couple of times. Since then she had begun refusing anything to drink so that she wouldn't need to go to the loo and she had got dangerously dehydrated in the early summer heat. She had swooned that morning. Then she had lost consciousness entirely when Ava was on her way back from school. The paramedics took her to the hospital and the doctors hooked her up to an IV and started to feed her saline.

'What's that?' Ava asked Pop when he got back from the hospital that evening looking absolutely shattered.

'Salt and water, love,' Pop answered. 'It'll see her right again. Replace what she's lost. Or some of what she's lost, anyway.'

They took Ava to see Nana the following morning. Mum and Pop stood outside the ward chatting with the doctor for a bit while Ava sat with Nana. She held her hand. It was mottled and wrinkled and colder than any living hand should ever be.

'Nana,' she whispered. 'It's Ava. Nana, it's me.'

Nana nodded very faintly. Her eyes lit up for the briefest second. Then they were gone again. Her lips moved but no sound came out. She was just going through the motions without anything to say. All those stories she had always told were bottled up in there.

No, that's not right, Ava thought. They were gone, fled. Nothing was bottled up in there. It was just emptiness, blank, nothing.

'Oh, Nana,' Ava whispered.

'Tut, tut,' Nana whispered. It was barely a breath. Ava leaned down to hear her better. Nana didn't look at her. She looked through her but managed to croak a few words at least.

'Don't be scared, Evelyn,' she breathed. 'The crows are watching. Nothing truly forgets.'

'It's Ava, Nana,' Ava said, but Nana didn't seem to hear her. Then Nana drifted off to sleep. She closed her eyes and her breathing went soft. Her chest barely rose or fell.

Ava picked up her schoolbag. She opened it and reached inside and fished about, found the necklace. Dustin's crow necklace with its feathers and bones. She placed it beneath Nana's bed.

'So they bring you back, Nana,' she said. 'So they bring you home again.'

Come on, she thought of the crows, to the crows. *If*

you're going to help her then now's the time. Make good on your promise, hold up your end of the bargain.

Mum and Pop looked a little more relaxed as they drove home.

'It's good news, love,' Pop said. He turned in his seat and winked at Ava. 'Your nana's vitals are all getting stronger now she's got the IV in. The dehydration knocked her for six but it's done no lasting damage. They reckon she'll be home in a few more days.'

That was something, then.

Nobody spoke for the rest of the journey. Mum put the radio on and Ava thought of Robin singing. She thought of Nana's words.

The crows are watching. Nothing truly forgets.

It had better be true.

Thirty

Ava sat with Pop in the living room. The evening sun cast a warm glow through the windows as it readied itself to set and he stared into the middle distance, ignoring the telly. She picked up the remote and switched it off and looked at him. The lines of his face cut deeper than normal.

She reached out and put a hand over his. He flinched and looked down at her, clearly woken from a reverie.

'It's OK, Pop,' Ava said.

'Oh, Ava, love,' he said. His voice was hoarse. He coughed and cleared his throat. 'Goodness me, I was off for a minute then, lost in my own world.'

'Are you OK?'

'Of course. I'm always OK.'

'Yeah, but you know. Really.'

'Really?' He looked down at her and smiled sadly. 'No, love, not really. I've never been so scared in my life. My heart is breaking, I think, watching your nana going through what's happening to her.'

'Yeah,' Ava said. She stared at the wall. 'It all seems so pointless in the end.'

'Love?'

'Life, you know. When you see it disappearing. Like Nana. Like . . .'

'Your dad?'

She nodded, blinked hard as her eyes stung.

'Yeah,' she said again. 'It makes you wonder what's the point in it all, in life.'

'No, love,' Pop said quietly. 'No, that's like asking a screwdriver to have a point. It has a job. You can use it. But it doesn't have a point. Well, to me, life is a tool, just like a screwdriver. A thing you can use. And you can use it to build or to break, or whatever else really. Just use it well and don't let it rust, don't let it go to waste. That's unforgiveable, that . . . letting it go to waste. Your nana taught me that. Nobody knows it more surely than her, or at least she used to. Use it well, your life, you old fool, she used to tell me, so I did. I built a home and a family. Your nana, your mum, you . . . and I'd say I've used it well, in the end.'

They sat quietly for a little while. Ava leaned in towards Pop and he put his arm around her and pulled her into himself. She stayed there for a long time, nestled into him. Pop's shoulders trembled slightly. It was tiny at first, barely noticeable, but it grew. It grew and Ava realized that he was quietly crying.

Thirty-one

The hospital called the next morning with good news. Nana was being discharged, she was OK to come home, they said. Her vitals were stable, just like Pop had said. Whatever that meant. Her memory still wasn't great, but that was to be expected. Her heart was stronger, at least.

Nana was sitting up in bed when they got there. She looked at Ava and smiled.

'About time, Evelyn!' she said.

Oh no, Ava thought. She heard Mum's breath catch. Pop just chuckled gently to himself.

'Behave yourself,' he murmured, and Nana winked.

'Only joking, love,' she said. 'I know my own granddaughter when I see her.' She paused and smiled wryly. 'Most of the time, anyway. Corbie's not taken everything yet.'

Ava stepped forwards and then near enough fell into Nana's lap, holding onto her. A sudden burst of emotion broke over her, fear for Nana, fear for herself, rage at the world ... and sadness. Just sadness for what Nana had been through.

'Oh, love, oh my love,' Nana said. She held onto Ava and stroked her hair with her gnarled fingers, her rough palms. 'It's OK, love, I'm coming home. They've got me back on my feet. It's all going to be OK.'

They got her home and up to her room. The journey exhausted her, no matter how well she said she felt. Pop and Mum helped her up the stairs and Ava went in front of them opening doors. She pulled Nana's duvet back and Pop lay her down to rest.

'Just forty winks, a bit of shuteye, let me dream of the crows,' Nana murmured. 'Then I'll be right as rain come teatime.'

Pop and Mum left. Ava stayed a minute as Nana held onto her wrist.

'Thank you, love,' Nana said. She passed Ava a little plastic shopping bag. Dustin's crow necklace was inside.

'It helped me more than any doctors' medicine,' she said. 'I found it, held onto it, and came back to myself. Oh, I was so far away, but this showed me the way back. The shadows got out of my way and I saw the path home.'

'The path through the woods,' Ava said quietly.

'Yes, love.' Nana smiled at her. 'The path through the woods.'

She fell quite quickly into a light sleep. Her eyes flickered behind their lids. Her eyelids themselves were paper thin. Like she could hardly keep the world out, Ava thought. Or like she could hardly keep it in, perhaps. Ava sat and watched her for a moment. She held onto Dustin's necklace. She still needs it, she thought. She still needs something to guide her back home.

She left it in the little plastic bag and slid it under the bed, just beneath where Nana lay.

'Come home again, Nana,' she whispered. *Show her the way*, she whispered in her head, thinking of the crows.

Thirty-two

The school hall was nearly full as pupils and parents and friends all found their seats. It was sleepy and stuffy and warm and more than one person found themselves nodding off as the performers came and went on the stage. Luke Jenkins came on and simpered through a couple of songs and one man started snoring loudly until his wife elbowed him in the ribs. Ava found her own eyelids growing heavy. Corbie whirled through the music. Her eyes closed and he cawed. Nana's face rippled. So did Dad's, vague and blurred. The air in the hall shimmered slightly with the ghosts of Crawford's long dead as Ava half-dreamed.

Then Robin came on. Ava sat upright, awake, alert. The world was alive. Mr Barnes played the first few notes and Robin adjusted the microphone stand and took a breath and everybody was transported away. It felt to Ava like they were all transported into their own memories, their own pain and sadness, their own exultant joy. Every memory was a story and every story was a part of each individual person's soul and Robin brought it all to life.

Robin sang for Jay, jubilant. Ava had heard the first three songs before. The fourth was new. It began with the lyrics *'A friend in pain, her father gone, she'll be OK, love's never gone . . .'* It was about Dad, Ava realised, and her heart soared. Her eyes misted up slightly as a lump rose in her throat. Deep melodies spoke of hardship and heartbreak. High notes danced above it all, happy and excited. Every range, every emotion, every thought and feeling ever thought or felt. Robin sang through them all, through their memories, their stories, those of every person in the audience.

Everyone stood as one at the end and roared and clapped and made as much noise as they could, bellowing for life. Jeanie and Phil were at the front, weeping and cheering. Robin blushed crimson beneath her heavy make-up.

'Oh, Robin,' Ava whispered.

Parents stood around afterwards drinking strong smelling coffee and talking about how great Robin was. Everywhere bustled with the heat and the crowd of bodies. Robin came out from backstage beaming and Ava held her tightly and she held Ava tightly, though she was quickly whisked away. Jeanie and Phil wanted her. Everybody wanted her. She was the star of the show. The other performers were congratulated too. It had all gone well. But the buzz and excitement followed Robin.

'What a night!' Robin said a little later. 'Wasn't it good! Wait . . . was it good? Really?'

'Yeah,' Ava murmured. 'Really. It was terrific. You were terrific. And Robin, that song . . . you know . . . about my dad. It was about him, right?'

'Yeah,' Robin replied. She blushed a little. 'Did you like it?'

'I loved it.'

Thirty-three

The solstice came and went. Nana seemed subdued.

'The longest day,' she muttered. 'They get shorter now. The days shrink around us and get darker. Always the way, always, always . . .' Then she drifted off further and came back less often.

Shadows clung to Nana and began spreading through the house. Everywhere Ava looked they seemed to be gathering, growing thick. The last day of school rolled around and the shadows were there in her room when she went to bed that night. They crept across the floor from the skirting boards, nestled under her bed, whistled from behind the curtains. *You're being silly*, she told herself. But they kept on coming.

Ava slept uneasily. Her dreams were dark that night.

Corbie whirled through the air, turned, and dived down at her. The shadows parted before him. They clung together in his wake. Nana was there all of a sudden and her eyes glowed bright and then brighter still. Ava heard a knocking sound from far off, hurried footsteps. The noise grew, insisted upon itself.

'Love! She's gone again!' Mum cried.

Ava was awake and up in an instant. Mum and Pop were crashing about on the landing outside her room.

Nana.

She jumped out of bed and quickly got dressed and rushed outside. 'When did she go?' she asked. Mum and Pop were heading downstairs. Pop was white with panic. Mum looked shaken, too. She turned at the bottom of the stairs and looked up at Ava.

'Half an hour ago, maybe,' she said.

'I woke up and she was gone,' Pop said. 'I was only up an hour ago and she was there in the bed, dead to the world.'

They ran out into the street, the same as last time, and they split up and hurried off around the block to try to catch her before she got too far. Ava looked all about.

A crow settled on a tree branch on the corner, white

feathers flashing in its wings. *Come, come,* it seemed to say. Then it took flight, flew a circle, and headed off.

Ava followed as the crow led her towards the blackforest. She sprinted across the meadow on the way up to the treeline. She knew where she was going, knew how it was going to end. Though, she admitted to herself, she was still pretty nervous. She was scared to go into the blackforest in the darkness, scared of what she knew she would find in there.

More crows gathered. They whirled around and glared down at her.

'It's time?' Ava asked them.

They all cawed. *Aye, little one. It's time.*

She headed into the woods. The crows were with her. They flitted through the boughs, through the shadows. They carried the shadows, cloaked her in them, and her heart began to beat harder and faster. They took her up along the slim woodland trail to where Dustin had always held his ritual. The hollow of earth, the thick fir branches, the cairn. There were no clouds in the sky and moonlight and starlight picked it all out clearly as Ava broke from the trees' cover. The hollow smoked lightly. Embers burned, glowed within it.

Dustin was waiting for her in the fire's light. He kicked a couple of branches aside so that more smoke rose and more light flickered out. His eyes were calm and still and he held his skull-topped staff in one hand.

'I knew you'd come,' he said.

Thirty-four

Something sat cooking in the flames. Ava looked closer and saw a couple of birds on a spit.

'They're not . . .'

'Crows?' Dustin barked with a cruel laugh. 'So what if they are? They eat their own. If you're to be believed, that's us, now, isn't it? Me, at least. Half crow.'

'Seriously, Dustin, what are they?'

'Birds. Who cares?' He gestured to a couple of small logs. 'Sit,' he said. 'It's going to be a long night.'

'My nana—'

'Is fine. She's fine. She knows these woods better than most. And she knows the old stories. They'll keep her right. That's what my mum always said.'

'She's forgetting them.'

'You never forget completely. Now, sit.'

Ava sighed. She glared and sat down and faced the fire, watching the birds cook. Their flesh was hissing and spitting, turning dark as the flames lapped at them.

'The food I gave you ran out?' Ava asked.

'This seemed more honest in the end,' Dustin replied.

'So this is what you've been living on?'

'When I'm lucky.'

His change was nearly complete. She saw it clearly right then. Half crow indeed. He had been living in the wild and the wild had well and truly seeped into him. He seemed, if anything, more beautiful than ever, she thought.

'It's the crows,' he said. He caught her looking and nodded as though reading her thoughts. 'They've finally begun to share with me since I've been living out here. I flew away and they found me.'

'You've heard them, then?'

'Heard them, yes,' Dustin said. 'Spoken with them. To them. As was always going to happen in the end, I think. I just needed to get out here, clear my head, so that I could listen properly.'

His demeanour had changed. No, not changed. Just

become ... more. He was like Dustin but more so. A natural and wild energy radiated from him. It had always been there, she knew it. But it had come to the foreground, now, grown far more potent, more powerful ... just more. A force of nature, Corbie come to life, Ava thought. In him, through him. Dustin was calmer with it, like a great sense of peace had settled over him. Like he had begun to shed the rage.

The crows perched on the surrounding trees and on the grass all around, just outside the firelight.

'Do you still believe it?' Dustin asked evenly. 'That there's no point?'

She smiled and looked around at the dark shapes watching them. She thought about Nana. She thought about Robin most of all. And she shook her head. No, she didn't really think it, not when she was in her right mind, when she wasn't so miserable. There were just some heavy burdens that came with it, with life. And that was OK. It was all part of it. There was plenty out there worth living for, plenty of furious, beautiful life blooming all around them, to make it all worthwhile.

'No,' she said.

He nodded and then he spat into the fire.

'You've changed your tune,' he said.

'I think we've both changed.'

They lapsed into silence for a while. The fire's crackling filled the space between them, casting flickering shadows on their faces. The odd flutter of wings danced around just beyond the fire's light. The odd caw.

Dustin had his sleeping bag with him, tattered and caked in mud. He threw it around his shoulders against the night's cold. He had a metal flask of water from which he kept drinking. Ava pulled her jacket closer about herself. Then after half an hour or so Dustin grunted and stood up.

'They're ready,' he said, nodding at the birds. He jumped down into the pit and picked them up by their spits. He got a couple of flat stones and lay them before himself and Ava, then dropped a roasted bird on each.

'Let them cool a bit, then we eat,' he said.

The thought of eating the bird meat made Ava feel sick. She was used to meat being sort of disguised. It didn't look like an animal when you got it from the shop, more like chunks of ... well, food. Proper food. Not like this. She sat there, half in the shadows and half in the firelight, staring down at the charred, burned bird, and she didn't know how on earth anybody could ever eat such a thing.

Dustin tucked into his gladly. He was a predator. He reminded Ava of dinosaurs she had seen in films, velociraptors and the like. Or, really, just sharp-beaked birds tearing into carrion.

'Eat,' he said quietly. He swigged from his flask then went back to silently ripping through chunks of meat with his teeth.

Ava picked up the warm, greasy meat, closed her eyes and bit down. She gagged as she sank her teeth into it. It was tough and dry, despite all the fat sizzling in the fire. She had to fight to get a proper bite. But she managed to get the first mouthful in, then a second, taking from what she assumed was the breast. It was cooked through and, actually, once she got her head around it, it wasn't as bad as she thought it would be. She took a third bite, then a fourth.

Something played at the edge of her sight as she ate.

'Yeah, you'll see it,' Dustin said as he saw her looking around. 'Always do out here. I do, anyway. These days, since I took to the wild.'

Flickering images danced in the shadows. Ava felt

like she was rising through the tree canopy. Then she was soaring. Her mouth felt hard as a pecking motion formed out of the darkness. She tasted mud and loam, then something sweet and slimy. A worm, perhaps. Then more flying, a bath in a deep, cold puddle, then adrenaline as something came at her, pain, lancing and sharp. Then something battered her hard and the shadows grew thick, stole the sight from her completely.

'Memories,' Ava whispered. She looked at the meat, the bird. 'The bird's memories, its last ones.'

'Memories,' Dustin agreed softly. 'Visions. Of a better world, a purer one. A wild one.'

'No,' Ava replied. She looked up as the trees around the clearing rustled. 'Visions of what's important in *this* world.'

Dustin grunted and smiled to himself and kept eating. A couple of crows broke out from the darkness and circled around above the fire. Another flew straight as an arrow and landed next to Ava. Then Nana came, shuffling out from the treeline, out of breath and looking like she was half asleep and dreaming. She was a bit bedraggled, with twigs stuck in her hair. Her eyes were wild, unfocussed. She was wearing her dressing gown and a pair of old wellies. The dressing gown was torn in places and the boots were covered in new mud.

Dustin's necklace of bones and feathers was hanging around her neck.

Ava leaped up and ran over to Nana, the meat forgotten, Dustin Marr forgotten, and clasped her to herself.

'My love, my dear, sweet Evelyn,' Nana whispered. 'I've come. I've come to get my soul back. I've come for my memories.'

Dustin stood and wiped the grease from his mouth with a sleeve. He brought a small bag from his pocket and tipped some bones from it into his palm.

'It's all ready for you,' he said.

Thirty-five

Dustin walked up to the pit as Ava and Nana both sat down beside it. He threw the bones into the fire and grabbed the branches and moved them to cover it all. The light dimmed. The shadows grew bold and crowded in from the clearing's edge.

Dustin held his skull-topped staff in one hand.

'You have come for the crows, to hear what they have to say,' he whispered. 'But the crows' words aren't for everyone. They are powerful memories, memories of the land and sky. The crows only choose who they choose. And who they choose must submit to them or be struck down dead. Soul dead. Do you both agree to the crows' terms?'

Ava and Nana nodded.

Dustin began to walk his circle around the fire pit. He walked behind Ava and touched his sooty palm to the top of her head. Then he carried on and passed them both a few times before stopping behind Nana. He kept his hand on her head and she kept her eyes closed, peace written on her face.

'There will be memories or death at the end of this,' Dustin said. 'You have chosen to come here. Do you wish to hear the crows' messages?'

'Yes, dear, I do.'

'Do you swear to listen or else be struck down?'

'I do.'

Then he walked around to Ava and placed his hand once more on the top of her head and repeated himself.

'Do you swear to listen or else be struck down?'

'Yes, I do,' she replied.

'Into the flames with you both, then.'

Ava and Nana both climbed down into the hollow together as Dustin drew a couple of branches aside. He took Nana's hand as she sat at the edge and lowered herself down and kept her firm, steady. Ava jumped in after her and the heat and the smoke washed over her. Nana sat against the pit's wall with her legs out in front, leaning against the earth. Ava sat next to her, just touching her. Dustin threw some fresh bones on the fire and then put the branches back. The fire popped and crackled. More smoke billowed through the branches' leaves and needles.

He chanted, 'Corbie, corvus, corvie... Corbie, corvus, corvie...'

Then his voice faded and the stifling heat took hold of Ava and made her head swim. Everything went dark as she sat there bathed in heat and ash...

She woke up alone in the hollow. It was cold and dark and she climbed out of it and looked up and saw Dad standing quite simply before her. He shimmered slightly in the bright moonlight and then grew solid. The logs on which she and Dustin had sat to eat their meat were still there and he walked over to them and sat down on Dustin's. He smiled at Ava, the same smile as ever.

Ava did nothing. She didn't move or speak. She just stood there like a statue and watched her dad, drank him in, saw the lines of his face and the way the starlight and moonlight played over him. The crows all stood around just as still as Ava. Some watched her, others him.

Dad.

Then Corbie, with his one eye and his white feathers in his wings, appeared from amongst the trees. He wheeled around the clearing and landed between Ava and Dad. He eyed them both and then began to sing, croaky and hoarse. The other crows called back in response.

Dad chortled and the crows fell still.

'Funny friends you've got here,' he said. 'Good friends.'

'I don't think so.'

'Oh, love. Don't be too hard on them. They did what they had to do, stayed true to their nature, just like you've done.'

'I don't know.'

'I do, and I'm so bloody proud of you I could burst.'

The crows took off, then, laughing, and left them.

'I don't get them,' Ava said.

'No, I doubt many people do. But that's OK. And look,' he held his hands out, gestured to himself, 'they gave us this little treat. Well, a big treat. They let us see each other one last time.

'And so, anyway,' Dad continued, 'enough about the birds. I want to hear about you. What've you been up to, love?'

Ava glanced back at the hollow.

'Me and Nana . . .'

'Ah, Nana.' Dad saw the look on Ava's face and he smiled again. 'Don't worry, love. She'll be OK. Her time will come, but it's not so bad.'

'No?'

'No, love. Not so bad at all.' He looked around. 'I never thought I'd see you up here, getting lost in these woods.'

'We moved to Nana and Pop's.'

Dad nodded. 'A good place to be.'

'And I'm not lost, Dad.'

Dad's smile broadened.

'No, love. I don't think you are,' he said.

His eyes the same as Ava's own. They glimmered as he watched her. He was so much like he had been in life, though not quite. Something was missing.

He nodded again as if he had read her thoughts.

'Just a shadow now, or something close,' he said. 'A memory, a piece of what I was. A piece of the soul I had, maybe. But that's OK. There's strength enough in that.'

'I know,' she said.

And she did. She could see it.

It was OK.

Dad's smile dropped, then. He looked serious.

'That Dustin Marr you're knocking about with,' he said. 'He's got a foot in my camp, a foot in yours. Especially now. Half in life and half in death. Perfect for old Corbie. But you need to put the crows and all that out of your mind for a little while, and soon enough. Life, love. That's what it's about. Until it isn't, but that's a way off. For now, it's all about life, you know?'

'I know.'

Dad's smile came back. It split his face and wrinkled his eyes. He laughed and his eyes sparkled.

'Oh, love,' he whispered. 'It's good to see you. So bloody good. My beautiful girl.'

Ava walked forwards and reached out and took Dad's hand. She was surprised to feel how solid it was, how real. Their fingers linked and they sat together. Time seemed to stretch.

There was so much that Ava wanted to say as the minutes ticked on. Her grief, her depression. The toll his death had taken on everyone. Everyone. And Nana. Most of all, Nana. She looked up, though, and saw his eyes, those eyes so much like her own, and she smiled. She didn't need to say any of it.

'I know, love,' he said quietly. 'I know.'

Then he just looked at Ava for a while and Ava just looked at him. It seemed to last for ever, them just staring, drinking each other in.

'They came for me when I died,' he said at last.

'The crows?'

'Of course.' His smile faltered ever so slightly. 'They came from everywhere, wings black as night and eyes sharp enough to pierce straight through me. I remember thinking those words, exactly, which was odd. It's not like me to be so poetic!'

He chuckled.

'They surrounded me, a dozen of them, but I knew ... I knew they weren't there to harm me. I was dead, after all. What harm could they do? Rather, they were there to guide me. And they did a good job of it.'

Ava sat frozen. 'Guide you where?' she asked, though she already knew the answer.

'On,' Dad said. 'To the next place. I walked and they flew all around me. They asked questions at first, all sorts of questions, and I answered them. They wanted stories, asked for them, so I gave them. Then after a while they didn't need to ask anything. I just kept talking and talking, all those stories pouring out of me. Every memory, every joy and regret. And with each word I felt a little lighter, as though my life's weight was being stripped away piece by piece. In the end I was almost empty and able to float freely. They brought me back to see you, but even now I feel that lightness tugging at me, my soul wanting to break apart and be free.'

Dad sighed and he looked at her.

'They're good, love,' he said. 'Good. And so are you. Brilliant. Blooming brilliant.' He gave her one final grin.

'You'll be just fine, I reckon.'

Thirty-six

Ava climbed out of the hollow. The air was as sweet as ever before in its freshness. Something inside her felt well, profoundly well, and she smiled quietly to herself.

'Dad,' she whispered, 'oh, Dad.'

The blackforest was all noise around her. Dustin was by his cairn with a flint in his hand. He had written fresh words in the stone. MIRIAM SHEPHERD.

Nana wasn't out yet, Ava realised.

Sometimes the ritual would be over quickly. Whoever it was would come out shaken. Sometimes it took longer and they would stagger out covered in soot and ash and quivering all over. Ava knew this. It didn't make it any easier as she took a seat and waited though. Nana took a long time. The longest time. Ava glanced at Dustin, but he stood unmoving, unmovable as he stared into the shadows at the clearing's edge.

What if she doesn't make it?

'Dustin,' Ava whispered.

He turned, furious, and held a finger to his lips, but Ava wouldn't be silenced.

'She's old,' she carried on. 'She's sick, weak. We need to get her out.'

She made to move towards the pit, but Dustin stepped in front of her and put his back to the hollow.

'You bring her out before the crows are done with her and she'll have to choose death. She'll be soul dead.'

Soul dead. She was already soul dead, Ava thought. But she could die for real if she stayed down there any longer.

A couple of branches began to move over the pit before she could reply, though. One of Nana's gnarly old hands came out, soot black and trembling. Then the other came out and Dustin went to her and helped her out. She was shaking, stumbling, shuffling. But she looked up and her eyes were bright.

'Ava, my love,' she said. Her voice was hoarse from the smoke, but it was strong like it had been when Ava was younger. 'I remember,' she said. 'Oh, love, I remember.'

*

They laughed a great deal afterwards. It was odd to Ava to see Dustin laugh like he did then, almost carefree. But then, she thought, it was odd for her to be laughing like it too. She hadn't laughed very much at all over the last couple of years. Now she could hardly stop herself, like she was somehow making up for lost time.

They sat together beside the pit, all three of them ashy and smoke stained. Dustin built the fire up to a roaring blaze so that the shadows fled.

'That's them told,' Nana cackled. 'Run, you pests, run away! We're in the light, now!'

Ava thought about what Dad had said. She'll be fine. Nana will be fine.

Ava rested her head on Dustin's shoulder at first. His animal smell clung to her as he put his arm around her. Then after a bit she snuggled into Nana, like she needed a bit of babying. She felt a little lightheaded and drained from all the laughing.

They ate the last of the meat.

'Best meal I've had in a long time,' Nana said. She looked around the clearing, at the cairn, at Dustin. 'Good on you, young man,' she said. 'You've got a heart of darkness, I can see it. But you've got a good soul. I always saw it when you were younger. It's why I tried to teach you while I could. Never let them tell you otherwise.'

The sky began to lighten as the fire finally burned down to a few glowing embers. Rosy fingers stretched out over the hills.

'Go down into that pit and grab me a handful of cold ashes,' Nana told Dustin.

'What are you doing?' Ava asked.

'Something very important, love.'

Dustin gathered the ashes and came back up and held them out to Nana in his cupped palms. Nana took his flask, poured a dribble of water into the ashes, and dipped a couple of fingers into the dark paste it all made. She daubed the paste around Dustin's left eye.

'Close,' she said, and he winked his eye shut. Nana smeared more paste around the eye, onto it.

'Open,' she said. The sun peeped over the horizon behind them. They all cast long shadows as they stood there in the dawn cold.

'Corbie indeed,' Nana said as she looked at Dustin's darkened eye. She took the crow necklace from around her neck and hung it around his. 'Or a good approximation, at least,' she carried on. 'His spirit in you, boy. It's over to you. A foot in life, an eye to it. And one in death. I'm just sorry it all had to be so difficult. That was never my plan.

'And, boy, something important, very important. You lived with such rage and violence in you, yes?'

Dustin nodded. He closed his eyes briefly, both of them. Then he opened them and looked at Nana as she carried on.

'You'll never get rid of it, that rage. I see it in you still, smouldering away just below the surface. But I think that you've come to terms with it, learned how to live without letting it control you. Yes?' Dustin nodded briefly once more. Ava could see it. He had grown calm, serene. Nana was right. The anger would always be there, but the violence was gone. He was in control of himself, not the rage.

'Good, good,' Nana said. She smiled warmth at him. 'You have accepted all that life is, made your peace with it, and so you are absolved. You are free from all that was, so that you can look forwards. Keep the stories, keep the town's soul. And don't cock it up, OK? I nearly forgot it all.' She jabbed a finger into his chest. 'You're better than that and I've always known it. *Always.*'

Dustin nodded and Nana turned to look at Ava.

'Now, my love,' she said. 'I should very much like to see your mum and Pop with my own eyes. Unclouded and fresh. Open. Imagine that! Open eyes and memories with which to make sense of it all. My soul complete. Come on.'

Thirty-seven

It was like they were coming back from the dead. The three of them walked from the blackforest as the sun fully rose, lighting them from behind so that their shadows continued to stretch out before them.

People came running as they walked down across the meadow. Mum and Pop came running. First they were terrified, then they were furious, and all the while they were overjoyed. They were overjoyed as they looked at Nana, and that joy trumped all in the end.

'My love, my beautiful,' Pop whispered as he held her hands.

'Hello, you old rascal,' Nana said. They kissed, they hugged.

'Mum?' Mum asked.

'In the flesh,' Nana said. 'And in the soul, too, more importantly. My love, Evelyn.'

There were plenty of other people there, too. Eileen Marr was there. She shared a brief look with Nana, a nod and a small smile. Then she and Dustin looked at one another for the longest moment and stepped in close. She fell into his arms and he fell into hers. She cried and he held her tight, his eyes shining. Both eyes, the one facing death and the one facing life. Then Dustin and his mum turned their backs on everyone else and walked away without a word.

He flew away, Ava thought. And he came back again. He was free to go wherever he wanted.

Robin and Jeanie and Phil were there too. Robin ran up to Ava, jumped on her, held her close.

'Oh, everyone was so worried,' she said. She stood back and wiped tears from her eyes and stared at Ava. 'I wasn't worried, though,' she said. 'Not for a minute.'

'No?'

'No. I knew you'd be OK. You had the crows with you, didn't you?'

Robin wiped her eyes with her sleeve. She met Ava's eye again and they both began to laugh.

'OK,' she said. 'I was a *bit* worried.'

The police were there, shaking their heads. Relief, exasperation, irritation. They had sniffer dogs with them who were beginning to prowl the edges of the blackforest up towards the river. The river itself had a police boat on it with a couple of people in diving gear.

'Quite the fuss we've made,' Nana said. She bent down to whisper into Ava's ear. 'I'm a mad old coot. What's your excuse?'

She winked and they both began to laugh again. Mum just shook her head.

'What did Dustin Marr do to you?' people asked. The police asked. A few others asked. Mum asked it quietly later on, back at the house, when it was just the two of them.

'Did he hurt you? Did he do anything to you?'

'No,' Ava said. 'We just ate some roasted crow, I think, and waited for Nana. Somehow we both knew she was on her way. Then when Nana came, we did Dustin's ritual and got Nana her memories back.'

'You *what*?' Mum asked. Then, 'You *ate what*?'

Mum shook her head. She looked exhausted and it seemed to Ava as though her brain was struggling to compute what Ava was telling her.

'It's complicated,' Ava said. But between them she and Nana managed to take Mum and Pop through it all. The ritual, all the ones Ava had taken part in. Ava told them about Dustin, about him being up in the woods, living wild. She told them that that was why the crows had come when Dustin attacked Luke. 'They wanted a way to get me to, you know . . . sell him out,' she said. 'And, I suppose, they wanted to keep the peace, I think.'

'No,' Nana said. 'They just wanted to keep things on their terms, at least until the boy was ready to listen.'

Nana told them that she had been called up to the blackforest. 'Old Corbie, the tease,' she said. 'Always up to mischief, poking his beak in, getting folks riled up . . . He brought me to you. Then I came round next to that fire with every memory I'd ever lost right there, flooding through me. God only knows how long I'll have them. I've no idea how much time I have left on this earth. Nobody does. But I'll make the most of every minute. Every minute, with all these old stories of mine up here.' She tapped her head and grinned.

'Oh, its brilliant. Brilliant.'

Mum and Pop sat watching the two of them with their mouths slightly open. They cried some more. Tiredness caught up with them all before long and they headed upstairs, hugged on the landing, then went their separate ways. Nana and Pop were gentle with each other as they went into their room. Pop held Nana's hand and Nana held him in her eyes. They shut the door to their own little world and Ava felt a great sense of peace settle over the house.

Thirty-eight

Nana died a few days later. It was peaceful and calm in the end and Ava remembered Dad's words.

It's not so bad.

They spent a lot of time all together in those precious short days before she died, though. Nana cooked a large dinner the evening after the ritual in the woods and they all sat around until late, chatting and laughing. She and Pop had more energy than anyone. They hiked up into the blackforest the following day, into the hills, just the two of them. They spent every moment they could together, giggling like little children. Even Mum joined in. She and Nana went out alone one afternoon and came back all smiles and tears.

Ava and Robin sat lounging together out on the front

step not long after they had all come back from the blackforest. There were a few clouds scudding in a hurry across the sky. Robin watched them. Ava stared at the shadows on the floor. They were faint in the midday sun but she knew that they could always grow again. The shadows could always grow.

'Stop being so miserable,' Robin said.

'I wasn't being.'

'Hm.'

'Yeah, well.'

Robin paused and sat back and stretched and yawned. Then she looked at Ava.

'So, what happened up there?' she asked. Everyone in town had been asking the same. So far Ava and Nana had only told Mum and Pop. But Ava wanted to talk to Robin. It was only right.

'The ritual,' she said.

Robin nodded. 'I wondered if that was it,' she said. 'Makes sense.'

'Yeah? I don't think most people would think so.'

'I'm the only one who thinks a lot of things.' Robin shrugged. 'So, it worked, then? The ritual?'

'Yeah. Nana came back with her memories.'

Ava told her all about it and Robin smiled. She stretched again and leaned her head on Ava's shoulder and started to sing quietly.

'*Go sweetly now and dream, my friend,*' she almost whispered.

Nana took Ava out walking the day before she died. They walked through the town and up to the blackforest. Crows followed them sometimes. Sometimes not.

'They're busy creatures,' Nana said. 'With short lives. So much to do.'

Ava thought on Pop's words all those days ago . . . *Well, to me, life is a tool, just like a screwdriver. A thing you can use. And you can use it to build or to break, or whatever else really. Just use it well and don't let it rust, don't let it go to waste.*

'Yes,' Nana sighed. She looked at Ava as though reading her thoughts. 'It's easy enough to think there's no point. There may not be. But that's OK. We can still do a lot, achieve something meaningful, beautiful. We can still build, can't we?'

Her eyes twinkled then as she smiled at Ava. She sighed, happy in the sunshine. Then she stared for a long time at a couple of large crows pecking at the earth on the other side of a small ravine.

'We've always had stories about them,' she said. 'The crows. Ravens, too. Rooks, jackdaws, jays. All *corvidae*, all part of the same family. Just as they've always kept our stories and memories, so we've always made up tales about them. It's no wonder, of course. You get them all around the world. Everywhere. So everyone knows them and they know everyone.

'Native Americans talk about them a lot. Various tribes. Most, I reckon. Their creation myths often involve them in some way or another. The Haida people said that the Great Raven was the creator who first called Earth into being on the endless sea. Then he made people. He made people of both rock and leaf. Or tried to, at least. The people of rock were hard to shape. He never quite finished them. The people of leaf were easier to work with. The Great Raven finished them and set them free to roam the land. But before they went, he told them that they must fall one day like leaves and rot back into the earth, and so death was invited into the world.'

She sighed again. There was a fallen log by a small, bubbling brook, and she sat on it and closed her eyes, faced the beating sun. Light flared around her and she drank it in. 'Oh, what a world, what a beautiful world,' she whispered.

It was an almost perfect day. They went to Marge's cafe and Marge greeted them warmly.

'Oh, Miriam, it's good to see you out and about,' she said, and Nana grinned.

Then they headed home to Mum and Pop and spent the evening all together. Nana told her stories. Story after story, like she was in a hurry to get them out, to breathe life into them. Then she died in the night, as people do. Ava got up the following morning and found Nana and Pop in the living room, sitting together on the sofa. It looked like they had been there all night. Pop had tears running silently down his cheeks. He had his arms around Nana. She was cold next to him, though with her head resting on his shoulder she looked like she could be sleeping.

Thirty-nine

They didn't hold Nana's funeral in the church. Pop was adamant. He had a row with the town's priest. She had wanted it outside and he was determined to make it so. They burned her body in the crematorium and then they all gathered by the river leading up to the blackforest.

Ava and Mum and Pop stood together. It seemed to Ava like the whole town had turned out as a hundred or more people gathered behind them. Robin stood next to Ava, linked arms with her, held her. Dustin lurked at the back behind everyone else.

Eileen Marr was up at the front with a couple more women all dressed in grey. There was a plain wooden table before them. Nana's urn sat on it, a small, black thing with her ashes inside. Candles and incense flickered and fumed in the breeze and a photo of Nana was propped up behind it all. She smiled. It creased her face, lit it up.

Eileen seemed nervous, terrified of all the people in front of her, but she took a deep breath and made herself speak.

'We're here today to honour our sister, Miriam Shepherd,' she said in a loud, clear voice. A couple of crows flew overhead. More gathered around the edges of the congregation.

Pop cried silently throughout. So did Mum. Ava just stood there staring at the urn.

They told stories of Nana. Eileen Marr did. The other women dressed in their plain grey clothes did. Pop went to the front and spoke at length. Stories and stories and stories. Then they lifted the urn's lid as a strong breeze picked up. Mum went forwards and took the urn and tipped the ashes out. Released them. They caught in the wind and flew away, whipped up towards the blackforest.

Nana had fixed Ava with a hard stare that final evening before she had died. 'The world around us,' she said. 'The *natural world*. That's what it's all about, love. It's precious, more precious than anything. That's what these stories all boil down to, isn't it? Don't lose touch with it. Learn from it, the hope and beauty it contains, see the power we can find in the unbridled, immeasurable, sheer amount of life around us. Blooming life. Terrible, wonderful life.

'Don't forget, my love. Don't ever forget.'

'I won't, Nana,' Ava had replied.

'Life, Nana,' Ava whispered as those ashes caught and whirled away. They billowed like a flock of birds and the thought made her smile.

She had realised a lot in those last few days, a lot at the end. What was the point in life? A foolish question, she realised. Or, at least, foolish to say that there was no point, to ask the question in despair when there was so much that went into living that life having a point or not became irrelevant. It simply *was*, and it was *so much*, and that was reason enough to cry aloud with joy. What did she have? She knew. It was so much. She had the love of her family, and the ability to love them in turn, a wonderful friend in Robin, memories of Nana, memories of Dad, Dustin, strange and wild. She had the future, unpredictable and full of life as it was.

Life. Terrible, wonderful life. That's what she had. It's what they all had.

'I won't forget, Nana,' she whispered. 'I won't forget.'

Acknowledgements

I am grateful for a lot in life, people most of all. For my family, for being who and what they are; for Bella at Guppy Books, a stalwart champion as ever; for Hannah, who helped me to beat the *Crow Children* manuscript into shape; for Taylor, who brought the crows to life; for Nelson, in a passing conversation with whom the idea for this book first came about; and for Lauren most of all, who brings clarity in a world all too often full of noise.